Lobo

The baby-faced outlaw with the lightning guns and the king of the horses were together that first day when Cody Quinn rode down to the great valley and changed it forever with his sunny smile and deadly .45.

Mitch Reece was just a horse rancher but after the young outlaw broke jail, leaving the marshal dead in the dust, he knew it was his duty to take the high trails in pursuit. He also knew that before it was done either he or the wild boy would be dead.

By the same author

The Immortal Marshal
Get Dellinger
Two for Sonora
One Last Notch

Lobo

Ryan Bodie

A Black Horse Western

ROBERT HALE · LONDON

© Ryan Bodie 2006
First published in Great Britain 2006

ISBN-10: 0-7090-8146-4
ISBN-13: 978-0-7090-8146-3

Robert Hale Limited
Clerkenwell House
Clerkenwell Green
London EC1R 0HT

Typeset by
Derek Doyle & Associates, Shaw Heath
Printed and bound in Great Britain by
Antony Rowe Limited, Wiltshire

CHAPTER 1

LOBO

He looked like just some harmless range kid – at a distance.

That was what deceived rugged Joe Henry, gun-guard on the Waterson Stage that came climbing up through the late afternoon dust to reach the watering stop of Morgan's Flat.

Henry, a big bearded fellow who allegedly slept with a sawed-off shotgun, was by nature twice as suspicious as the next man. Yet even he didn't scent anything amiss as Jed Clump wheeled the coach up to the way-station and hollered for the hostler to come hold the horses.

The slender youth lounging on a log bench on the shady side of the station, chewing a straw, barely glanced up at the sounds of hoofs and wheels.

Federal Marshal King Brodie, staging across the territory on official business, would have certainly been alarmed had he caught a good look at that face, but there was no chance of that until it was too late, due largely to the fact that the young 'kid' seemed to keep his face hidden in the shadow of his Stetson hat. Another factor was that the dapper federal lawman was still diverted by the prettiest stage passenger he'd encountered in a coon's age.

Her name was Carrie Clarke and she was returning home to Rimfire after completing her formal education in the east. During the long run up from River Wells she'd chatted pleasantly with the hard-jawed lawman and was pleasant to the pair of drummers lounging untidily in their seats opposite.

Despite this diversion, the marshal was far more an expert on outlaw faces than pretty ones, and would have surely come up with both guns in his fists had he been granted one clear glimpse of that young man's face before everybody stepped down to stretch their legs and wonder where the hell the hostler was. But this did not happen and the four passengers, driver and shotgun-guard were well away from the coach and four before the young man in the yellow shirt suddenly looked up sharply and stared across at them.

'Hey!' Joe Henry called. 'Where's Cheeney?'

The man rose silkily, shrugged his shoulders and began to make his leisurely way across forty feet of hardbaked dirt towards the stage. He was smiling beneath his tip-tilted hat and was supple and graceful in the way he moved. He packed a tied-down .45, but that was the norm rather than the exception in this country. 'He migh' be catching forty winks,' he drawled. 'You know, hot day and all?' They studied him more closely now. He wore crossed shell-belts around his hips and walked like somebody who loved every moment of life: jaunty, energetic, lithe-moving, and it was plain to see now his body had the sleek look of uncommon speed and strength.

Suddenly the marshal's instincts began to kick in, some-thing about the young man ringing a bell in his brain. With a muttered curse, Brodie stepped well clear of the girl and his right hand reached towards the sixshooter hanging from his belt on the right side.

'Don't commit suicide, Marshal!'

Brodie stared – then allowed his big black gun to slide back into the leather. For the stranger had drawn faster than it was possible to follow. Yet there was no denying a black gun muzzle was now trained directly on the marshal – and he was cowed. Not so Joe Henry. Henry had two disadvantages the lawman lacked. He didn't know who the young man was, and was hot-headed and impetuous by nature. Disregarding the threat of that naked piece, he cursed savagely and made to jerk up the riot gun in his big rough hands.

But the boy in the yellow shirt plainly anticipated trou-ble and was lunging forward at incredible speed before the shotgun had barely moved. He reached his man with time to spare and his gun barrel cracked viciously across Henry's wrist, then whipped up again to clip the side of his skull with stunning impact.

The big man reeled away and the stranger went after him to pluck the weapon from his grasp before smoothly kicking his legs from under him to bring him to ground. To Joe Henry's shame, he began blubbering.

'Feel proud of that, do you, Quinn?'

Everyone stared at the marshal, who'd spoken. The bearded driver gaped, turning pale as he backed up a pace.

'What are you sayin', Marshal? Is this—'

'Sure,' the young man said lazily. 'I'm Cody Quinn.' He winked at the girl. 'But that don't mean I shoot up everyday folks for fun . . . or take a kiss without asking first.'

'Cody Quinn?' she gasped, and for the first time that day Carrie Clarke's composure threatened to desert her. 'You . . . you couldn't possibly be that . . . that outlaw!'

The man-boy bowed from the waist and smiled. His face had a youthful handsomeness dominated by wide-spaced blue eyes and a clean and determined jawline.

'I'm afeared it is so, miss,' he conceded. Eyes with little chips of steel in them shifted focus to the glowering figure of the marshal. 'You were almost too smart just there, Brodie. I didn't count on you recognizing me so quick.'

'Seems I was still too slow.' Brodie's jaw was set in grim lines. 'All right, where's the agent?'

'Inside sleeping it off. The tap on the head I gave him, that is. So, now we're acquainted and time is running short, what do you—'

'When did you break out of Shattuck Range?'

The young man's unlined face hardened.

'I busted out when I was good and ready is when. Now close up all of you, and you listen to me, star-packer. What I want from you is a little information on what's going on down below where you just came from today. Yeah, Alameda. I got it on good information my mustang's down there still and that mean-mouthed old sonova Venture has got him hidden away someplace. I just want to know if that is so or if it ain't. Not complicated, is it?'

'You mean . . .' the girl said, astounded, 'all this is about some stupid horse?'

'Easy, easy,' the outlaw admonished, his smile flashing white. 'Some Westerners can be mighty touchy about their cayuses, miss—'

'That mustang doesn't belong to you and never did, outlaw!' the marshal cut in angrily. 'Sure, you might've ridden it a spell after the bank job when we were after you, but that was only after it got separated from Mitch Reece, the rancher that is. Mitch owns that mustang, outlaw.'

'A hoss belongs to any man who's got the guts to claim him and the grit to hold on to him, badge-packer!' Suddenly Cody Quinn looked and sounded much more than any boy. 'After I lost him in the Shattucks the night Reece nigh ran me down, he must've headed back to the rangeland. I heard the whisper that that stinking old back-shooter found him then hid him away so's Reece wouldn't find him. Matter of fact, the whisper is that the sheriff's been sighted riding him about when he thinks nobody's a-lookin'. So, just let me know if I've heard right about all this and then I'll be on my way . . . honest Injun.'

Six sets of eyes stared at him, first in suspicion but then with a growing conviction that he seemed to be speaking the truth.

'Go straight to hell—' Brodie barked, but the shaken driver spoke over him.

'What you just said could likely be true enough, boy. Everyone says that wonder-hoss is around Alameda some-place but nobody seems to know just where. Mebbe you know how sly and secretive our sheriff can be. Now are you gonna let us get on and. . . ?'

'You're free as jaybirds,' Cody Quinn said amiably, convinced he'd heard the truth. He removed his hat with a flourish and bowed low to the girl who almost looked amused. 'I gotta say that at times like this a man wishes he wasn't on the dodge and might come calling on a pretty woman without worrying that the law, the government and the whole US Army mightn't come howling after him. But who can tell? Mebbe we'll meet again in better circum-stances one day?'

To the astonishment of all, including herself, the girl heard herself say, 'I certainly hope so, Mr Quinn.'

'Right obliging of you, miss,' he smiled. 'Would I be pushing it to ask your name?'

'I'm Carrie Clarke.' She hesitated, then added, 'I've just finished college back east and am on my way home to join my parents in Rimfire.'

'Rimfire, eh? Well, could be I might just come calling one fine day, Carrie Clarke.' He laughed. 'Cross my heart, I promise I won't show up at your folks' door with half the county tagging me, looking to lynch me.'

'Are you really an outlaw? You don't look. . . .'

'Old enough?' he finished for her, and a sudden youthful laugh sounded. ' 'Course I'm not. I'm no outlaw, blue-eyes. Folks just gave me a bad name is all, and you likely know how that can stick.' His smile faded and he approached the girl and held out his hand, which to the astonishment of the onlookers, she took without any sign of apprehension. 'I'll change what I just said to a promise. I will come calling on you some fine day soon when the dust is settled some, Miss Carrie Clarke. . . .'

'Damn you, man, will you leave that girl alone,' King Brodie protested. 'It's outrageous enough you bailing us up this way without you—'

'You call this bailing up, Brodie?' Quinn cut in. He shook his head. 'No, this is just stopping by for a quiet talk. If I ever bail you up, badgeman, you'll sure as shooting know you've been bailed.'

With that he backed away, covering the ground with surprising speed. He went to his horse, dozing in the heat, swung up and vanished into the woods without having a hand lifted against him.

Instantly the men began cursing and threatening to get

a posse together as soon as they reached the next town. They rushed into the station and released the trussed-up agent, then eventually set about preparing a meal which was consumed to the sounds of increasingly louder and braver talk.

The only one who didn't join in all the overheated conversation was college graduate Carrie Clarke, who seemed lost in her own thoughts. Out of nowhere, a handsome young rogue had ridden into her sedate life and whether he was an outlaw, as they claimed, or a killer like the marshal insisted, she knew it would be a long, long time before she could forget what those blue eyes had looked like in the sunlight.

They were coming!

Mitch Reece knew it long before the two hands he'd brought with him up to Silverado Plateau in the pre-dawn darkness came alert. That was understandable. For they were just working hands from his spread and in no way obsessed the way he'd always been about the wild ones.

The horse rancher had chores aplenty awaiting his attention back at the spread stretching from here to there, yet here he was back in the wild upper-Shattuck country twenty miles from home in the pre-dawn chill just for one reason and one only.

To see them.

And suddenly they were close – or so that gradually rising grey dust-cloud on the far western rim of his vision told him.

The wild mustangs, the mares and stallions and foals that ruled Silverado Plateau, the maverick untamed lords of the wilderness, were, for a man like Mitch Reece, right at the top of his list of the most wonderful critters on earth.

Flowing across the limitless high country reaches as they had been doing for longer than anybody knew, hoofs hammering, uncut manes and tails flowing in their back-draft, running for the sheer joy of it because it was what they did and what they could never stop doing. Except, of course, when someone skilled like him might set a trap, take his catch back to the plains, break them to saddle and bridle and then sell them for cash before he grew too fond of them. Now they were drawing abreast of Reece's look-out blind, streaming by in an endless torrent, these descendants of Arabia by way of the Spanish plains of Cordoba centuries ago.

These horses carried within them no psychic memory of their European homelands. They were American horses streaming across the American high country in exactly the same way they had done for centuries, sweating backs gleaming in the early light, eyes bright with arrogance and pride; the freest most exciting spectacle Mitch Reece could ever witness.

And just as quickly they were gone.

'Well,' the rancher said after the earth had stopped trembling and he had a fragrant cigarette going, 'what did you think? Worth the ride up?'

The hands were impressed, but were not nearly effusive enough to suit their boss. Not that he gave a damn really. He'd promised his new hands he would bring them up here to get a look for themselves at the prime source of the spread's income. But that had just been an excuse. Any time he might be feeling low, a simple ride up here to country could set him up again for the next week, the next month.

On the way down he was thinking about the finest mustang stallion he'd ever roped and broken . . . before it had been stolen by wild Cody Quinn and eventually vanished altogether.

The one named Lobo.

The horse was king in most of the vast new lands west of the Mississippi, but in Esmeralda County it had come to rate even higher to become in many an instance the measuring stick which a man, a town or a people were rated by. A good horse got a man respect. An exceptional one might get you invited to join the exclusive Cattleman's Club, while a genuinely extraordinary cayuse could – as it had actually done one citizen who owned a prize-winning horse – get enough people to vote for you to get you elected to the county council.

Then came Lobo.

The wild mustang stallion of Silverado Plateau had generated a name that had come to border on the legendary long before Mitch Reece finally managed to achieve the impossible and caught it after an extraordinary chase of more than a hundred mountain miles.

Experts raved about the horse's strength, speed, cunning and staying power, yet it was the stallion's appearance that initially caused strong horse-lovers to go weak at the knees.

An easterner might sight the stallion and see only a small horse with a dusty dun hide, an odd-coloured, stringy, long mane and tail – nothing special about him at all. Yet another who knew something about horseflesh might note the depth of chest and the prideful glitter of fierce black eyes. But the expert was always mesmerized by the head and neck, for it was there that the ancient Spanish bloodlines manifested themselves so dramatically, but only to the eye of the true connoisseur.

The big head that appeared outsized joined the short

breedy neck like the two sections of a hammer, perhaps a hammer poised ready to strike.

The head was held high and that arrogant stare radiated authority, a pride and an intelligence that had survived even after Lobo had been caught, tamed and broken to bridle and saddle, a process that had taken Mitch Reece longer to complete than with any other horse he'd ever handled.

Now that proud wild head was lifted high and the horse stood motionless in flooding moonlight as a shadowy figure approached silently through the trees flanking the sheriff's hidden back-canyon rancho, ears pricked, the whites of the eyes yellow in the light.

There had been no sound, no alien scent, or nothing untoward to be seen. And yet such were the senses of the once wild horse leader that Lobo knew that there was something or somebody out there in the shadows that had not been there before, and he swung his arrogant head in the direction of the cabin for a sign that the man he hated may have also detected whatever it was that had alerted him. The cabin lay locked in silent darkness.

The sheriff always slept well out here along Spring Creek, for the good reason that scarcely anybody knew about his hideaway in the cottonwood-choked back canyon.

Even before the sheriff had caused Mitch Reece's prized mustang to 'disappear' during the turmoil of the manhunt for Cody Quinn months ago, the lawman of Alameda had increasingly felt the need of a hideaway from his many enemies. This was due partly to the number of natural enemies he made legitimately, along with all the people he conned, injured, falsely accused or otherwise offended.

Sheriff Venture could be more of a two-gun rogue than many of the badmen he brought to book, here in a county which by and large was ill-served by most of its lawmen. But because his record against the ungodly was so impressive his masters at the capital chose to turn a blind eye to his excesses.

So an ugly old man slept with an easy conscience and secure in his hidden hideaway, as the kind of danger that might even turn his greying thatch pure white, were he aware of its presence, ghosted through the trees not fifty yards distant making no more noise than a passing zephyr.

And only the horse heard the whisper, 'Hey . . . there you are, old pard. Reckoned I'd gone off and left you to fend for yourself forever, did you?'

The horse trembled and stepped quickly to the rails of the corral as a lithe figure ghosted out of the deep gloom of the woods, nostrils flaring, poised ready to run yet instantly half-recognizing the stealthy nightcomer now ghosting towards him, small booted feet making no sound in the dew-damp grass.

Lobo whickered softly.

This was no ordinary man approaching the corral, and Mitch Reece's wild stallion was about as far removed from an everyday saddle-horse as might be found anyplace.

Pure mustang from head to toe, the horse Reece named Lobo was anything but pretty with its dusty dun color, the big hammer-head mounted on a short, breedy neck, the clean, neat trimness of steel legs and the depth of chest that spoke of a huge heart and lungs that never failed.

The moment recognition hit, Lobo emitted a sound of pure pleasure which was cut off when a slender hand slipped through the railings and closed its mouth.

'Easy, easy, old fella. I know you're pleased to see me – just as I know that mother-loving old lawdog is likely as deaf as a post and at least halfway blind. But let's do this nice and quiet . . . we can get to celebrate later. What do you say?'

When he took his hand away the mustang stood in total silence watching the slim figure cross to the gate.

Fifty yards distant beneath his high corrugated-iron roof the most feared and successful peace officer in the county's history slept on undisturbed, dreaming of all the badmen he'd led to the gallows and those yet to be pursued, caught, accused, tried, convicted then swung high, wide and handsome to join the twenty or thirty old Venture had already hurled into eternity.

But listen!

A faint sound almost penetrated the outer fringes of Herb Venture's unconsciousness. It was the sound of a gate creaking open as his most prized possession was led from the corral across to the stand of brush where Cody Quinn's saddle-horse was tied up.

The lawman groaned and full sleep claimed him again. He would not awaken until daybreak when he would throw the worst temper tantrum his deputies had ever seen, which was going some.

All Esmeralda County would have been agog to know not only what mysteries were unfolding here in the tall timber country five miles east of Alameda, but also of the events leading up to them.

Everything centered around outlaw and bank bandit Cody Quinn.

Several months earlier Quinn had plundered the Rock Creek Bank of Rimfire of twenty thousand in cash and made it as far as Alameda before the robbery was discovered and before his shot-up horse fell dead underneath him.

Despite a reputation for bravado there was no way Quinn was going to show up afoot with a big yellow leather valise stuffed with one-hundred dollar bills at three in the morning in the home town of outlaw-killer Venture.

So instead he'd tramped two hours across country to reach the horse ranch of respected citizen Mitch Reece where he used his unique horse skills to select the rancher's most prized possession in the mustang Lobo, and was ten miles away riding like the wind with his twenty grand strapped to his saddle in back of him before sunrise.

The stallion carried the outlaw to his secret eyrie high in Shattuck Range but later picked up a stone bruise on the runout and Quinn stole another mount. Naturally Sheriff Venture and Mitch Reece headed up manhunts, and it was at that point that what was known and what was merely conjecture became blurred. Everyone knew the bank money was never found, but what had befallen Mitch Reece's prized mustang remained something of a mystery.

Everyone knew Lobo had vanished; but where?

The truth of it was Venture had calmly and criminally elected to keep it.

The horse affected men that way. It had affected Quinn badly, and he'd deeply regretted having had to discard him during his flight. But Quinn had his contacts, his instincts and his famous good luck which had all played a part in his tracking down Lobo – finest damned horse he ever threw a leg over in a lifetime.

Now he'd searched, found and was gone.

Nobody seemed to give a damn when Venture rode into Alameda next day in an apoplectic rage, which the

17

lawman could not explain for to do so would have been to admit that he had indeed – as some rumour-mongers had it – recovered Reece's wonderful horse months earlier and had 'chosen' to accommodate it at his spread without informing its rightful owner.

But he did reveal someone had allegedly been sighted astride a horse that resembled Reece's 'missing mustang', and eventually mustered a reluctant posse to go search for it.

Mid-morning found the Sheriff of Esmeralda County riding miles out along the north-east trail searching for sign. But upon returning empty-handed to Alameda later, Venture was informed by the stage company of an incident involving a Waterson stage up at Morgan's Crest the previous day.

Witnesses, including Federal Marshal King Brodie, attested that the robber of the Rock Creek Bank was back in the county after a three-month exile.

That had been two hours earlier now but gnarled and lethal Venture was still in a simmering rage as he cut a fresh mount out of the jailhouse corral and commenced packing his warbag.

Nothing would now convince him Lobo had been stolen by anybody other than his youthful *bête noire*, bank robber and enemy of law officials everywhere, Cody Quinn.

If this were so, then Venture vowed not to sleep until he had the mustang stallion back in his possession, but whether or not the lawman-cum-horse lover would return Mitch Reece's property to him should that eventuate was anything but certain.

Initially, the manhunting sheriff had been too enraged at the theft of the horse to find any sign worth a damn. But during the hours he forced himself to put in back at the spread now, somewhere around mid-afternoon in a damp creek bed a few miles north-west of the cabin, he jerked his horse to a halt and jumped down to stare at the footprints in the mud there.

Small as a woman's, neatly booted, they were instantly recognizable as the footprints he'd once searched for in vain up in Shattuck Range for weeks after the Rock Creek Bank robbery.

Once certain Quinn had been the thief, he did a curious thing. He dismounted by the trickling stream, filled a foul-smelling pipe with shagcut and puffed his way through it before finally nodding in satisfaction and getting to his feet.

The horse-thief had ridden north-west. That encompassed a huge area of Esmeralda County, too big for any man or posse to cover properly.

But Herb Venture wasn't just a foul-tempered old crowbait of a country lawman. He was smart and well informed, particularly on the subject of criminals and their associates.

Right at that moment, Venture would have been ready to wager big money that he'd just figured out exactly where his wonderful bronco and that baby-faced bastard of a horse-thief had gone.

The sheriff froze on bringing the Rooney ranchyard into sight.

Sheriff Herb Venture was in his fifty-eighth year but old age was already upon him. He had slowed down in mind and body. His eye was growing dim and his trigger finger had lost its quickness, leaving him with little left but courage, cussedness and a reputation for bringing in badmen.

Yet glimpsing Mitch Reece's magnificent half-wild mustang stallion there in George Rooney's yard that night caused his heart to leap inside his chest and he felt almost like a manhunter of forty-five again as he cocked the .45 in his hand and ghosted towards the darkened ranch house.

Venture had dismissed his posse after experiencing his 'revelation' concerning Lobo and his suspected thief. He'd headed north-west alone, continually considering and reconsidering his hunch about Quinn's whereabouts, and continually arriving at the same answer; Rooney Ranch.

Rooney and the kid went back a long way. It seemed Rooney had helped Quinn out once when he was just a kid, and he'd later repaid him by backing the rancher's play with his sixgun in a range war. He believed they'd maintained contact ever since, but doubted if Rooney or Quinn realized he knew of their ongoing close friendship.

So he'd ridden thirty miles directly to Rooney Ranch headquarters, and upon finally sighting 'his' hammerhead quietly munching hay in the corral he'd congratulated himself then settled down to wait.

He was a master at this sort of thing; the Territory jails were full of hardcases who'd underestimated his skills and ferocity of nature.

He chuckled in triumph. With all the wide west to roam, Cody Quinn had come here, just begging to be taken.

But the most dangerous thing a man could do when dealing with someone of the kid's calibre would be to rush things. You could get killed that way. Instead he kept watch from a deserted barn directly across from the corrals until he'd caught that sudden glimmer of nocturnal movement across the yard.

Now he turned his back upon the mustang and his stalking shadow merged with the great dark mass of the house and all was quiet again on the ranch of George Rooney, pioneer, cattleman and, perhaps unwisely, long-time friend of Cody Quinn.

The sheriff knew the layout of the house, knew exactly where the spare bunk room was situated off the rear gallery – the room where he expected to find his man sleeping like a baby and waiting to die, by his gun.

Herb Venture hated the outlaw kid but nobody knew how Quinn might feel about the badgeman. And even though now back in Venture's bailiwick and with half the Territory on the lookout for him by this, Cody Quinn was still sleeping soundly at the spread for over an hour before being awakened suddenly, not by conscience or any sense of impending danger, but rather by simple hunger. In retrospect, the past twenty-four hours culminating in his stealing back 'his' prized mustang and making it safely to Rooney's spread, seemed almost too easy. After he'd ridden the mustang hell for leather across the thirty miles to reach the Rooney Ranch, he'd then sat up for hours talking and laughing with George and his boys, too excited to think of food until a growling belly interrupted his sleep.

The very first thing he thought of was that forequarter of smoked ham he'd sighted in the meathouse earlier.

Armed with his bowie knife and wearing only faded Levi's with a pistol thrust into the waistband, he made his lithe, light-footed way along the smooth boards of the gallery, thinking only of what he'd do to a solid one-pound chunk of good meat, his soul off watch.

He was in the meathouse two doors down when Herb

Venture eased up to the wide-open door of the guest room and poked his .45 barrel round the doorframe.

Moonlight filtered through the window and the sheriff's long bony jaw dropped an inch when he sighted the mussed and empty bed.

Even so, he was infinitely wary as he eased his rawboned frame deeper into the silent room, for this outlaw kid had a reputation for slipperiness, low cunning and gun lightning second to none.

But the bedroom was plainly empty as Venture stood at the bedside staring down at a pair of flashy-looking boots parked neatly by the bedside table, and his mean old heart seemed to catch in his mouth upon sighting the double gunrig hanging from the bedpost like something reptilian; motionless yet sinister. One holster was empty!

So where was the bastard?

Gone like the wind at some instinctive whiff of danger as had happened so often in the past?

For a bad moment Herb Venture gnashed tobacco-stained fangs and envisioned what the press would say if Cody Quinn, whom they loved because he sold papers, had given him the slip yet again.

Then he heard it. A low, tuneless whistle in the stillness followed by the soft padding of bare feet coming towards the room.

Old and creaky or young and limber, the sheriff of Alameda had always been at his deadly best whenever the chips were down.

Two quick backwards steps took him into the dark little space between the clothes closet and the wide-open door. He crouched shrouded in blackness as the whistling faded and a slender figure suddenly halted a foot short of the doorway, totally motionless and backdropped by the New

Mexican moonlight pouring down over George Rooney's garden.

Cody Quinn didn't appear to breathe.

A young man with a lifetime of violence behind him, he was part unrepentant outlaw, part animal. Primitive instinct dominated in that split-second as he stared into his room, the sixgun filling his hand with a speed which almost caused the man crouched in the darkness to gasp.

'*Quien es?*'

Cody's voice was sharp with a suddenly aroused sense of danger. He couldn't see properly, having just come in out of the moonlight, but his sense of smell and hearing were working overtime as he stood motionless, bowie and meat in one hand, cocked .45 in the other.

He held the sixgun upright against his chest, ready for instant use. The temptation to angle the weapon forward then lunge after it and start in blasting might have proven too strong for another, but not 'the kid'. He knew the moment he moved foward without visibility he could provide a sitting target for whoever might be waiting for him there in the darkness.

'*Quien es?*' he snapped out again.

The sheriff didn't even breathe as he recognized the voice. That damned kid right enough! His heart hammered as he waited for the other to make the suicidal move of showing himself, then cursed his own stupidity. This son-of-a-bitch boy badman had likely packed more gun experience into his twenty-whatever years than he had done in his fifty-eight. There was no way he would come from moonlight into a darkened room when instict warned him there was something amiss.

Venture the manhunter was untroubled by ethics, conscience or any foolish sense of compassion as he reached a lightning decision and raised his gun barrel. A man could get killed here if he didn't act fast and do it right. Which meant kill the little bastard before he maybe gets a sniff of danger and kills you! Within mere feet of him was the outlaw who had escaped lawful custody twice in Esmeralda County; had robbed and plundered and built up a kind of cult-following amongst the low-lifes of the Territory even before he relieved the Rock Creek Bank of $20,000 before vanishing unscathed yet again.

Born to die.

Faster than blinking, Venture's gun arm snaked around the door jamb and almost touched the outlaw's skinny chest in the blackness before he jerked trigger. The .45 exploded with an ear-splitting roar.

What the lawman did not see – had no time to see in that life-or-death split-second – was that Quinn was holding his Colt vertically against his skinny chest, ready to flick the barrel in any direction and open up in the shaved tip of a second.

He wasn't given his split-second of warning.

The explosion of Venture's gun was followed instantly by a ringing metallic clang. The lawman's bullet had struck the chamber of Quinn's revolver, hammering the breaking weapon against his breastbone with an explosive force that literally flung the outlaw backwards. Blood ran from the gunboy's forehead where his pistol barrel had struck him under the driving impact of the slug.

'It's me, punk!' Venture shouted, rushing forward to loom over the fallen figure with thick smoke spilling from his gun muzzle. 'Venture! I got you and I want you to take that into hell with you, you worthless little bastard!'

But somehow Quinn seemed able to stave off total unconsciousness long enough to whisper mockingly,

'Almost touching me with your shooter, yet still couldn't kill me? Why, you broken-winded old fart, you are even farther over the hill than I had you figgered. . . .'

Suppressing a curse, Venture cocked the piece again, was taking aim, deliberate as destiny, when the kid's white smile widened in the bloodied face.

'That's right, dust me off, old man . . . and the twenty grand with it. . . .' His eyes closed. He waited for the bullet that never came.

'Well done, Sheriff,' said the chief marshal from behind his desk. 'They say he will live, which at least opens the door on a chance to find out what he did with the Rock Creek bankroll.'

'Yeah.'

Venture could be as sullen and surly with superiors as with anyone else. In the aftermath of the night's dramatic events which had put his gaunt and craggy countenance upon the front pages again, his sense of triumph was muted by regret. It had been the lawman in him that stopped him hammering that bullet into Quinn's brain, yet the hard old hater in him was now bitter he'd chosen not to blow Quinn into hell when he had the opportunity.

They now had the outlaw locked up tight under a twenty-four hour watch in Rimfire Jail with a doctor and six marshals in attendance, and he would face trial for robbery and murder just as soon as he could stand in the dock up at the Rimfire courthouse.

This was good enough for the law but not for the sheriff. Not now.

For once again Quinn was the name on everybody's lips, and though Venture was receiving acclaim for nailing him, it was still not as good as it could have been.

In his mind's eye he envisioned a newspaperman's photograph. It showed a tall lean lawman with his five-pointed star clearly displayed on his chest, leaning on his rifle with one range boot propped upon a headstone whose inscription read:

CODY QUINN
SHOT DEAD BY SHERIFF HERB VENTURE
BURN IN HELL!

He sighed for the what might-have-been and creaked to his feet. At least he might still get the secret of the Rock Creek Bank stash out of the outlaw before he swung, although he didn't like his chances.

'Will that be all, Chief?' he growled.

The marshal rose and extended his hand with a smile.

'For the moment, yes. And once again let me express the appreciation of all law enforcement bodies in the Territory. And do try to cheer up a little, old fellow. You almost look as though Quinn got you, not the other way round, heh, heh.'

No answering smile flickered across his wintry visage as Herb Venture quit the roomy office to step into the street where the sun was shining and life was pulsing through the town of Alameda. So he'd bagged the kid! What kind of victory was that? He'd wanted to kill the lousy little scut! Still did.

The deputy was standing exactly as ordered alongside the two horses tied to the hitchrack. The sheriff's regular mount was a beautiful appaloosa, bred to run, to stay and always to look like the horse of an important man. By contrast, the runty mustang stallion was smaller, skinnier and appeared almost stunted at just fourteen hands tall.

And yet to the eye of a horseman, that mane and tail and maverick eye all said the self-same thing: champion.

His champion.

He now truly believed he had earned the right to claim the dun as his own, was prepared even to thrash that out with Mitch Reece if needs be. Possession was nine points of the law in this case, at least in the sheriff's head. That thought almost brought a smile, may have done so had not the reporter and cameraman come rushing up at that moment, notebooks in hand, barking questions about the kid.

Not a word about the kid's conqueror, mind. Just a whole mess of questions about that miserable little show-off now nursing the king of all headaches while languishing behind bars at Rimfire Jail.

The newsmen drew not one word from him as he swung astride his fine horse and wrapped the stallion's lead rope around his hand.

The photographer's camera went off with a flash of powder.

The newsmen couldn't understand it when the sheriff flew into a rage and demanded they destroy the negative. They refused to do it and eventually he was forced to offer them a bribe, which they flatly refused.

The sheriff's temper flared but he controlled it. Venture was forced to think ahead. He'd hidden the coveted stallion before and was ready to do so again. Mitch Reece had never tracked it down to his hidden spread before; he was confident Lobo should be safe out there with him again.

He'd lie to Reece if needs be. He was a really convincing liar.

Cheered up some at the thought, he decided it was

time to return to the spread which had become virtually his full-time base ever since the long-suffering Mrs Venture had finally wearied of his ways and returned home to Richmond, which was just about as far east as she could get from him without getting wet feet. Venture owned a fair piece of land back home and had rented a quarter section out to a man named Petrolle who ran sheep and goats and with whom the lawman was now feuding. Six months earlier Petrolle sublet his spread to another man then vanished for several months without explanation. This subletting angered Venture and roused his suspicions about Petrolle whom he was now convinced had a shady past. Petrolle was back but he and Venture wrangled constantly, the lawman's always prickly ways having calcified into open hostility over time.

Drawing close to his home acres, Venture encountered goats roaming free on his dirt, while smoke from his rented land indicated Petrolle was burning off, which in summer could be dangerous.

Still buoyed up by his triumph over a lethal adversary, the lawman decided it was time to get tough with Petrolle also, and kick his ass right off his land and to hell with whatever legal recourse the man might have. Or for that matter, just how truly dangerous that hard man might prove to be.

Mitch Reece was always pleased to return to Mustang Ranch and that day was no exception. Cupped by the rolling foothills of the rugged Climpson Range, the meadow valley stretched westward away from the stand of trees where he halted his gelding, from which point he could see where the spread was touched only at the very furthest tip by the stage road that ran from Rimfire to Madigan.

He stepped down and rolled a smoke, a tall and rangy Westerner with angular features bronzed deeply by the elements, and lined by hard work and commitment. But softened now as his gaze cut instantly to the horses dotting the grass below. Mustang was a horse ranch, and fillies and colts played below, racing across the meadow tossing their heads, testing speed and stamina against each other.

Cheeko River, which ran the full length of Esmeralda County, bisected the Mustang from north to south. Near the northern treeline where the river entered his valley, Reece could see the roof of his house through the trees, the barn just beyond.

Home was good even when a man was returning from what amounted to a failure. When Cody Quinn busted out of whatever nest he'd been holed up at in the range several days earlier, Mitch Reece had ridden up to the Range in the hope that the kid might still be in possession of his mustang, Lobo.

No luck.

Quinn had come by Lobo somehow before going on to the Rooney place where Venture had taken him in. But according to that mean-eyed old badgeman the mustang had bolted and nobody had sighted it since.

He'd just have to realize the horse could be gone for good and accept it.

Mary had breakfast on the table before he was back five minutes. Reece sat at the table in the bay window overlooking the east pasture where two of his men could be seen in the corrals breaking a filly. The smell of ham and eggs filled the house and Mary's eyes sparkled the way they always did whenever he came home. For he was away a great deal this rancher, hunting the wild horse herds, cutting out the quality animals that showed most promise.

Breaking and training broomtails was a punishing way to make a living, a living which he augmented by breeding Arabs for which there was always a ready market.

But the mustangs were his prime passion, and he kept glancing out to see how the boys were making out with the off-white filly which he had roped up in Claw Hollow just a few weeks earlier. Until his wife felt obliged to bring him to order.

'Mitchell Reece, you rush off in the middle of the night from my bed to go chasing yourself all over the Range; you're gone for days, come back dirty, unshaven and half-starved; I sit you down to a lovely breakfast and me, and all you can do is gape out that window. I swear sometimes I do believe you should have married a horse.'

'I did: the prettiest filly in New Mexico,' he grinned.

But from there on he paid attention.

After all, he loved his wife but was merely obsessed with wild horses.

She brought him up to date on the latest news but made no mention of Cody Quinn. As he ate, talked and drank his coffee hot and black with plenty sugar, Reece was unwinding, loosening the belt a notch, spreading long legs further beneath the table. Mary suggested he catch a couple hours' rest before he considered doing anything, and he was beginning to think maybe she was right.

A hand came in looking for something and Mary went to attend to the man, leaving Mitch to look around for the newspaper. No sign of it; she always left it on the sill of the bay window. He enquired about it when she returned to the room and started clearing off the breakfast things.

'It didn't come yesterday,' she said casually, heading for the kitchen. 'The mailrider must be on the bottle again.'

30

He accepted that. The mailrider was a famous boozer. Normally you could rely upon him to get your mails and stuff through flood or fire or acts of God, but when things got easy he was just as likely to uncork a bottle and you might not sight him for days on end.

Mitch rose, stretched, scratched his belly and yawned. He was reflecting idly on the weeks he'd put in combing the entire Crater region where Cody Quinn and his loot from the bank had vanished months earlier.

The heller had been up there all that time. Must have been holed up someplace safe laughing his head off as platoons of possemen, bank agents, lawmen, bounty hunters and optimistic locals went over Climpson Range with a fine-toothed comb. They claimed he was part man and part will-o'-the-wisp, and he guessed they might be right.

One thing was for sure now; they'd never sight Quinn in these parts again. And maybe it would be best that way; everyone could get on with their lives following the biggest upheaval the county had ever seen.

He was heading for the washroom when he saw it. Peeping from beneath a pile of folded towels was a corner of a newspaper. He tugged it out and frowned at the current edition of the *Rimfire Herald*. How could Mary have made a mistake like that?

He opened the folded paper and immediately had his question answered. Page one was dominated by a headline reading:

CODY QUINN CAPTURED ALIVE BY SHERIFF
VENTURE!

The article was accompanied by a photograph of the victor

of the Rooney Ranch gundown sitting his horse in Alameda with a mustang hitched to his saddle.

A quick step sounded. He looked up. Mary was frowning.

'I really didn't want you to see that, although I knew you'd find out sooner or later. I just wanted it to be later, I suppose.'

She knew what he would do. Mitch Reece knew it too.

CHAPTER 2

WRONG MAN
TO RILE

On the morning of July 5, Sheriff Herb Venture mounted the mustang stallion and set off along the dusty ranch track for his leaseholding in the timbered back canyon. He packed his iron as usual, for he was a man with many enemies, even here in his home county. Apart from that he was *en route* to deal with, once and for all, the ache in the backside that went by the name of Kip Petrolle. Petrolle's damned goats had gotten into his truck garden overnight.

Again!

There was a limit to what a man could take, and as Venture's boiling point was lower than most folks', he was primed ready for trouble right now and knew exactly what he intended doing.

Issue marching orders.

The sheriff spat sideways and the horse pricked its ears. He patted its silky neck. Tough luck, kid!

Venture bit off a chunk of chaw tobacco and ruminated on the outlaw kid. It had been just like Cody Quinn to mention the stash and thereby save his own lousy life. Everything the little bastard had done was clever and spectacular. He won gunfights which he should have lost. If he cracked a bank, as was the case at Rimfire, it turned out to be holding record deposits plus an overnight shipment destined for a major bank. And when he finally busted out of the Shattuck Range after three months in hiding, during which he was written off as dead, he did so astride a horse so full of running that the possemen never even saw which way he went.

Or what he did with that twenty grand, an inner voice whispered, causing Herb Venture to spit splashily again.

Naturally they'd searched the Rooney headquarters high and low without uncovering one dime of the Rock Creek bankroll.

The wounded gun punk had smirked in Venture's face when he'd demanded to know the whereabouts of the stash, 'Or I swear to God I'll blow your maggoty face off,' as he'd put it.

'Blow it out your ass, old man,' was the mocking response. 'You'll never see it . . . but you sure as glory will see yours truly when I bust out and come lookin' for you with the biggest knife in all the Territory. . . .'

The sheriff straightened his back and switched his thoughts to his share farmer. He'd had a bellyful of Petrolle and had finally made up his mind to be rid of the man. He could draw more pleasure from something like that than kissing a pretty woman between the breasts. With the possible exemption of that handsome brown-haired woman down in La Luz, he modified. And wondered if he might settle down and marry again when he finally hung up his guns.

The mustang danced along in the deep dust of the trail, hoofs unshod yet rock hard. Riding Lobo was like sitting a rocking chair, the sheriff was thinking almost pleasurably, when he looked up to see the buckboard drawn up on the trail a couple of hundred yards ahead.

Petrolle.

Venture recognized his tenant instantly. As he cut the stallion's gait back from a lope to the trot his sharp old eyes noted every detail of the other's attire – brown Stetson set squarely on the head, blue coveralls, ash-coloured jacket from beneath which projected the gleaming wooden butt of a revolver, a black-and-white knitted scarf around the throat against the chill which still lingered even though the sun was well up by now.

Tight hard lines appeared about Venture's eyes, and his lips flattened as he brought Lobo back to a walk. There was a touch of the dude about this fellow which, added to his rocky-jawed toughness and arrogance, had always caused Venture to be naturally suspicious of his background. When you added this to his damned marauding goats it combined to present a picture of one man he decided he could well do without from this day forward.

Petrolle's face showed no expression as the tall horseman on the likely-looking mustang halted alongside his buckboard. Solidly built with deep-set dark eyes and a long top-lipped duckbill of a mouth, Petrolle was blowing puffs of breath mist into the cold air. There was a travelling blanket across the man's knees. Finally, Venture was forced to speak first. 'You must've sensed I was coming to call on you, mister.'

'Why should I?'

'Your lousy goats, is why. They were in again, and I told

you last time what would happen. You're through, Petrolle. I'm hereby cancelling your leasehold. I'll give you 'til Monday to pack and clear off, not a day longer.'

'What if that don't suit me?'

Venture's eyes glittered as he rested a bony hand on gunbutt. 'You're still off either way.'

'Is that a mortal fact?'

In that moment, sitting tall in the saddle with one hand on his gun, Venture appeared little different from his younger days when he had first carved an impressive niche for himself in the annals of law enforcement.

Yet the sheriff was ageing, and not only were eye and reflexes a tad slower but also his instinct for real danger had lost a little of its razor sharpness.

His attitude towards this man was proof of this.

Kip Petrolle was loaded for bear. He was indeed, as Venture half-suspected, a man from the wrong side of the law, having escaped justice by the skin of his teeth from Arizona Territory to seek out a nice quiet hideout. Here he got to raise goats and sheep and let some old wounds heal. On the debit side was the sheriff-landlord who seemed to be forever harassing him over one piddling thing or another, and the last time it happened, Petrolle had told himself quietly it would be just that. The last time.

His blood was up. That day he was no longer a simple raiser of sheep and goats but a very dangerous man who was being pushed too far

He said softly, 'Why don't you get your broken-down old ass out of my sight before I let five miles of daylight through you.'

Venture went rigid in the saddle. 'Last warning, mister!'

'Go fry!'

Venture went into his draw. He was very fast for a man of his years, certainly didn't lack grit.

But Hickok in his prime might well have run a bad second that day against Kip Petrolle, and the .52 calibre Spencer rifle he was holding across his knees beneath the blue travelling blanket had his left-hand forefinger curled around the heavy steel curve of the trigger ever since Venture had looked up and sighted him on the trail.

Petrolle fired twice.

The first big slug drove through Venture's heart and out his back. The second struck him in the temple. Either shot would have proven fatal. He crashed to earth on his face almost under the forewheel of Petrolle's rig, his Colt out but unfired, a finger of the right hand still against the trigger.

The stallion danced for several paces then halted, nostrils flaring at the smell of gunsmoke. Petrolle wanted to pause and savour the spectacle of the vaunted lawman sprawled untidily upon the trail like one hundred and seventy pounds of dog meat, but knew it was a luxury he could ill afford.

He had killed one of Esmeralda County's more prominent citizens and suspicion would likely as not point to him.

Time to say goodbye to goat farming and long lazy days sitting in the sun with a pencil stub mapping out hold-ups. Luckily he'd planned on quitting and returning full-time to the owlhoot; he had places to go, people to see. And if he wasn't sorely mistaken, he also had just the sort of likely-looking cayuse to get him there best in crackerjack time.

'Here, boy,' he said, clicking his fingers and jumping down. 'Did I hear old aching-ass call you Lobo?'

Mitch Reece rode easy in the saddle as he drove his cavalcade of horses out of the timber to follow the winding trail
towards the river. Although he had every reason to reach
Alameda as quickly as possible, there was never enough
good reason for the horse rancher to run condition off
good horses. So he took his own sweet time and enjoyed
the mildness of this summer's day as he approached the
county line from the east.

Reaching into a saddle-bag he drew out a fat sandwich
of sliced beef and pickles and munched hungrily without
taking his eye off his charges.

He was herding thirteen geldings from Mustang Ranch
up to a client in the Schaefer Hills. The geldings, all sleek
and in tip-top shape, were bays and sorrels with just two
greys and a black, ranging from two to four years old.

His ramrod had intended bringing the horses to the
Schaefers early the following month, but when Mitch
suddenly decided he had urgent business to the west he
elected to handle the chore himself.

He might well be desperate to get to Alameda to check
up on Lobo, but he was still a horse-breeder rancher and
therefore always ready to mix trade in with anything else
that happened to be going on.

He followed the line of the hills as the trail meandered
its way to the river. The cavalcade clattered by a compound
of several old adobes and upwards of a dozen false-fronted
tents which made up the site of one of the new little boom
towns springing up all over out this way here on the very
edge of a wide and grassy plain. Behind this frail little
outpost, the mountains reared up; the horses showed signs
of skittishness as they approached the crossing but he

hustled them across without delay with a rope's end snapping at their tails.

The tumbling, rushing river of swift water boiled and burbled its way across the plain from the high country. He saw a big yellow fish break the surface in one of the deep rock bowls where the river backed up into quiet water.

Times like this a man felt free and easy no matter what might lie either behind or ahead. He liked the way the geldings looked as they frisked on ahead and he relished the way thoroughbred Regal Harkeef moved beneath him as the road began to rise and the smell of pines drifted in from the north.

They called the stud 'Reg' on Mustang Ranch but Regal Harkeef was his name on the pedigree. Mitch Reece had imported the stallion from England where it had done much to improve the bloodlines of the third Earl of Coventry's breeding stock. The big grey had done the same for Mustang's bloodlines. The more prominent characteristics passed down from the grey were graceful slender necks set deep in strong shoulders, muscular forequarters, deep through the heart area, short withers sloping into short backs and genuine thoroughbred's mainstay of the Reece-bred horses both here and in Mexico. The thoroughbreds paid the bills and gave Reece and Mary the good life they'd worked long and hard to attain, and he loved them as any horseman would, in particular big grey Reg who moved beneath him now like silk, ready to respond to the slightest command, eighteen hands of pure aristocrat.

Yet why would any breeder with his meadows already alive with fine young blood horses be spending time away from his everyday duties to drop off some stock at Candelaria then push on all the way to Alameda in search of a wild broomtail stallion?

The answer was simple.

Mitch Reece was a horse breeder but a mustang lover. Hunting and breaking wild horses had been his means of setting himself up in the horse business and getting himself a stake which he eventually parlayed into his own outfit. There was some profit to be made in mustangs and he certainly did so. Yet compared to the money to be acquired in raising blood stock, the wild horses side of his business was small, and from time to time someone who did not know him well might suggest he get rid of the 'rough stuff' cluttering up the spread and concentrate exclusively on the quality.

This he would never do.

There would always be mustangs on his ranch. He would always be ready to take off and roam their wild ranges up in the Shattucks, looking for a promising young colt or filly to rope and gentle – providing they didn't get to kick his head in first.

And there would only ever be one four-footed king of Mustang Ranch in his book and that king was not beautiful Regal Harkeef but rather a horse called Lobo. Reece's eyes shadowed.

It was well over three months now since an outlaw had infiltrated the spread on a moonless night to coax Lobo from his pen then vanish somewhere into the range astride him with a sack containing the sum of $20,000 slung across his back.

He'd not seen the mustang since but was looking forward to a reunion in Alameda.

Just on nightfall Mitch swung his little herd toward a steep-walled canyon that promised good bedground. He found water and sweet grass just inside the coolness of the canyon mouth. There was shelter amongst the trees for a good camp. The night passed uneventfully and mid-morning found him urging his charges into the stockyards at Candelaria where his client was waiting with his chequebook.

The urgency that he'd suppressed over two days took hold of him as he loped away from the high town to make his way back to the long grass plains at a swift pace to raise eventually the rooftops and the galvanized iron rain-catchers of the town in mid-afternoon.

It was at the imposing law office where the chief marshal presided over county affairs that he'd first heard that Sheriff Herb Venture had appropriated Lobo following the shootout with Cody Quinn, but then had himself been gunned down later in some crummy domestic dispute on his own land.

There had been no sign of the mustang stallion when the law arrived at the murder scene, he was informed by a junior marshal with the sniffles. The authorities believed the man responsible was a former Venture tenant named Petrolle who had vanished from the region, presumably astride the very animal in which Reece was interested.

The animation which had kept him fired up ever since learning of the Rooney Ranch shoot-up left Mitch in a rush as he slumped back in his chair.

As if it hadn't been enough to have Lobo flushed out then stolen by one lousy bank-robbing son of a bitch, it now appeared the horse had had the misfortune to fall into the hands of a sheriff-killer.

Yet when the first disappointment had passed he had to admit to himself that it was not all that amazing or coincidental when it was all boiled down. To any keen judge of horseflesh, especially if they happened to be men with a need to cover vast reaches of territory at optimum speed, a likely-looking prospect like Lobo would catch any and every eye.

Regal Harkeef would leave Lobo for dead over a short distance, but it would be the English aristocrat that wouild be humbled should the race continue for twelve hours or even twenty-four. A pure mustang of a certain breed and conditioning could seemingly run forever, which put such a mount beyond price for a bank-robber or lawman-killer on the run.

'Are you all right, Mr Reece?' enquired the junior marshal with the sinus condition. 'You look all played out.'

Mitch pulled himself together, got to his feet, turning his hat in his hands. 'No idea where this Petrolle was headed?' he asked.

'None. We finally dug up some paper on him from Alamogordo, though. Murder, banditry, rustling. You name it and he's done it. Why do you ask?'

Good question, Mitch thought. He'd once spent days and weeks searching for Quinn's hideout in the Shattucks, all without success. He was certainly not even thinking about taking off after some butcher who could be halfway across Arizona by now.

'No good reason.' He went to the door, paused. 'Is Quinn still alive?'

The marshal looked impressed.

'Sure is, tough little bastard. Some of these halfwits who admire him boast he can't be killed, and this is going to fuel them up. But the ninety-nine folks out of every hundred who know he can die, and can't wait to see it happen on the gibbet, are going to have the last laugh when he swings by his scrawny neck.'

'Nothing on the Rock Creek Bank loot?'

'Nary a thing. Won't say a word. But we've got people working on him, tough people.'

This brought a wintry smile from Mitch Reece.

'Hope they are good at their job. That robbery damn near ruined our county, certainly ruined many a neighbour and townsman of mine.'

'You can bank on it, Mr Reece, Marshal Gant's a specialist in squeezing out of dirty hardcases what they vow and declare they either don't know or will never tell.'

'I believe Quinn is pretty tough.'

'Not that tough. Marshal Gant could convince St Peter to tell him where God lived.'

'Glad to hear it.'

'Sorry about your broomtail, but then they're pretty much a dime-a-dozen, ain't they?'

'Not this one.'

CHAPTER 3

PETROLLE RUNS SOUTH

The back-country rancher was a hard-working and God-fearing man in his middle years, capable of making a success of raising cattle in a region of poor soil and meagre water supplies, and mean-spirited enough to make the lives of everybody around him a misery.

More often than not his prime target was his daughter whom he considered plain and dull yet who in truth was neither. Having long since driven wife and two sons away from Clifftop Ranch, and with his three hands inured to his tongue and ill-treatment, it was mostly the daughter who bore the brunt of his insults and bullying.

Today was no different. Except for once the rancher did not have to resort to comments about her appearance, incompetence or other imaginary failings, but felt he had something meatier to chew on. Namely, the sneaking belief that one of his hands may have passed on to his daughter some kind of message from the lowlands. He could not prove it but was intent on finding out. For that was how it had started with the missis. Notes at first. Then she vanished in the middle of one dark and stormy night riding his best goddamn horse and he'd never sighted her or her lousy lover since.

'You better hand it over, miss,' he growled around a jawful of greasy pork which she had prepared for his midday meal. 'You know you're gonna have to sooner or later, so why not make it easy on your stupid self.'

'More coffee?' she replied.

He swore at her. She made to get more coffee from the pot on the range and he hurled a chunk of bread in her direction.

'Sneaky, lyin' and ugly – just like your ma! Did you get a letter or didn't you? Hey, come back here, I'm talkin' to you, ugly-face!'

The young woman retreated to her room and bolted the door and leaned her back against it, eyes closed, lips moving silently.

She was a tall and brown-haired 28-year-old, settling into the primness of early spinsterhood. Already her face had taken on a set, slightly heavy look like her father's, a look which could degenerate into surliness if unchecked. She always covered her quite graceful tall body with heavy, unattractive clothing that made her look even more of an old maid. But today she was far from feeling attractive, maybe further than at any point in her unhappy life.

A note for her from Los Robles had been handed to one of the hands when in town the previous day.

She took it out and scanned it with eager eyes. It read:

COMING TO BE WITH YOU AT LAST.

It was signed K.P., which were the initials of the wild man she had met on a visit to her aunt in Weed some months earlier. Kip Petrolle.

At the time he'd vowed he was in love with her and would come up over the cliffs one fine day to demand her hand and 'deal with', as he had put it, her father should he attempt to stand in their way.

She pressed the slip against her straining bosom and looked at the ceiling. She did not know if she returned Kip Petrolle's hot passion or not. But that was secondary. What thrilled her was the awareness that Petrolle was treated with great respect up in Weed where he had the reputation as a genuine hard man and deadly with a gun.

She would rather have such a man come to Clifftop Ranch with his Colt buckled to his thigh, than the handsomest, wealthiest beau in Laporte County who might well buckle and run the moment he confronted her father.

True, she dreamed of love, a fine wedding and enough violent sex to send her grey inside a month. But even more longingly she dreamed of Petrolle shoving that big black gun of his in her father's fat belly and forcing him to beg simply to be allowed to live.

Petrolle stood by the dun at the long hitchrail, watching the town.

Weed was not much of a place, just a scatter of buildings that had grown up around a cattle camp and telegraph office. But it boasted a fine big saloon and a few men with money, one of whom owed the hardcase plenty. On the down side there was also a law office manned by a hard runt of a sheriff who doubtless by now knew all about Sheriff Herb Venture and the violent fate that had befallen him just two years short of retirement.

Petrolle's lips quirked.

Regret was a stranger to him. Yet even so, he doubted he would have plugged Venture had the ageing badge-packer been less of an arrogant old bastard. Venture had kept at him as though he'd wanted to see how far he could push him and get away with it. Well, now he knew. The sheriff was cold in the ground and Petrolle was on the dodge, as he had been so many times in his life, and every time had survived the experience.

At least this time he had a destination and the perfect hideaway spot, he reassured himself. Maybe that was what he had in mind when he played up to that brown-haired girl he'd met here on his last visit – thinking of the future hideout potential of Clifftop Ranch in the event he cut loose again and needed a spot to lay low.

For he would always 'cut loose', sooner or later.

He was a man who could go weeks and even months playing it straight, tipping his hat to the ladyfolks, keeping out of the way of men with badges on their chests. But sooner or later he would bust out, and there were dead men in graves strung across the Territory as testimony to the fact that when Petrolle cut loose it was time to run.

But deep down he was not sure that refuge had been the only reason for his decision to come here to this high country backwater.

Petrolle was hard and double-dangerous, but he had his softer side and had often found himself thinking of that tall woman in her lumpy clothes in an almost tender way over recent months.

He rubbed his arms. This was semi-arid land here and it could get cold at night, colder than in Alameda.

What he needed first before he went looking for a fat man with cash, was a drink. Something to warm the blood.

47

To sharpen his brain after hour upon hour spent crossing the big country.

The thought caused him to turn to the mustang. It stood streaked with sweat at the hitchrail but with that outsized head held proudly high and the breeze stirring mane and tail.

This time Petrolle's grin was easier. This damned broomtail had proven the finest four-footer he'd ever thrown a leg across. A running machine. Small wonder old Venture had gotten his hooks into it after blasting Cody Quinn. He wondered idly how Quinn had come by the critter. Not that it mattered, of course, outlaws did what they had to do. Cody's doings had seen him likely land on death row somewhere, while Kip Petrolle had managed to get himself in a shooting scrape, as a consequence of which towns, any towns, were dangerous places for him to be right now.

He chuckled.

He loved danger.

But in the event he might encounter more of that commodity than he was reckoning on, he judged he should take full precautions to ensure his safety.

The lamplit livery smelt of saddle soap, leather and horse sweat. He paid the boy a quarter to wash and curry the stallion, feed it a dish of corn and give its legs a massage if there was time for that before he got back.

The boy stared at him with his jaw hanging. The telegraph had hummed its news across the miles to Weed, and even pimply stable-boys knew Kip Petrolle was hotter than a two-dollar pistol right now.

'Get busy,' Petrolle instructed briskly, yet was sobered by the boy's reaction even so.

The telegraph might well be a boon to mankind but it

could be a genuine pain in the ass to a man on the dodge, sometimes. If a snot-nosed kid sensed he might be the killer they were after, he should play his cards extra close to his chest.

Better take the back streets to find the fat man.

But his man was no place to be found off the main street and eventually Petrolle was obliged to tug his hat low on to his hawk nose, turn up the collar of his jacket and hunch up like a deadbeat drifter before venturing back on to the main concourse which went by the name of Buffalo.

Buffalo was nothing but twin rows of rickety false-fronts blotting off a view of tumbledown frames and seedy rooming-houses. Travelling the boards, he encountered cattlemen, cowboys, sheepmen in greasy coats and hard-eyed *hombres* like himself just looking for trouble. He would settle for a shot then a glimpse of his debtor.

Petrolle eased his way between a pair of swaying drunks and entered the first saloon.

He surveyed the noisy scene from beneath his hatbrim, readying himself for what he was about to do. The fat man owed him over two hundred from a poker game. Normally he would have paid up by now. But being a shifty varmint he would know Petrolle was in deep trouble with the law and would likely lie low, hoping Petrolle might get himself killed in a gunfight before settling day came.

The bastard!

A square-shouldered figure stared at him from the smoke-shrouded bar and Petrolle felt a weakening run through him. It was that stinking sheriff with the parrot-beak snout. What was it about this country that made their lawmen so ugly and unlikeable anyway?

He found an empty chair at a table and dropped into it,

his back to the room. When he looked up the sheriff was gone and directly across the bar-room, emerging from an alcove, chubby cheeks gleaming with rude good health, was the player who owed him a double century.

Easing to his feet, Petrolle made his way past the dice men, the roulette-wheel jockeys, the faro hopefuls and those too broke to do anything but watch. The fat man was leaning his paunch comfortably against the edge of a keno table when he felt something ram into his spine and a tough voice whisper, 'You and me outside, Fatty. It's settling day.'

The fat man's eyes stood out like dog's balls as he screwed his thick neck around to take a look at what he could see of the square-jawed face under the Stetson.

'Er . . . ahh, anythin' you say, Kip,' he said, but he said it way too loud. Heads jerked up from the game and suddenly Petrolle was feeling about as inconspicuous as a cat with a new dog in the house.

'Kip?' some half-wit gasped, wide-eyed. 'That you, Petrolle?'

Time for action.

Seizing the fat man by the collar at the back, Petrolle whirled him away from the keno table and began hustling him for the side door. When the man began making a noise like a broken bellows and croaked for help, Petrolle plunged his hand into the man's pockets and came up with a fistful of notes, just as a citizen yipped and hollered, 'Hey, that's Petrolle right enough. What's he doin' with Luis?'

'Git the shurf!' the fat man suddenly managed to holler, and a moment later was driven face-first into the wall by the door under the impetus of a powerful thrust and a boot planted to his chubby backside.

Petrolle was gone in a flash and legging it for the livery.

He was as fast as he was tough but not fast enough to outrun the cry that sped ahead of him: 'Petrolle's in town!'

And then, 'Where is the sheriff?'

The answer to that was – close by. Real close.

Petrolle was within half a block of the livery when the man with the badge erupted from a diner off to his right, spitting a half-chewed chop from his mouth and clawing for iron.

Weed rocked as Petrolle and the badgeman traded lead in a short and savage duel until a near miss sent the sawed-off toting badgeman diving for dirt and cursing fit to kill.

It was a bareback Petrolle who stormed off through the back streets follow by outraged cries and the odd wild shot.

The mustang ran as though he were back with the mobs of Shattuck Range without bridle, rider or galloping pursuers in its dust; ran as though for the pure joy of it, flying through a night peopled by clumps of brush, the oddly human shape of cactus and small furred and scaled creatures which fled from its headlong path and stayed hidden as an angry man wearing a badge with a rag-tag-and-bobtail posse strung out behind him went churning by.

It was midnight before the glitter of Crystal Cliffs rose before Petrolle's eyes to loom high in the starry night. Atop the cliffs lay the rough acres of Clifftop Ranch, but the only access was on the southern side, guarded by the old Mexican town of Los Robles.

Los Robles was linked to Weed by that curse of badmen on the run everywhere, the telegraph.

Limping now, Lobo grunted as the rider sawed back on the reins to drag him to a sliding halt in the grassy sand at the toe of the cliff.

Petrolle gazed upwards then behind. He could not see the possemen at this point but could hear them faintly as they clattered across a sweep of hard earth he had put behind him maybe ten minutes earlier.

Ten minutes. . . .

He jumped down and realized the horse's offside hind leg was streaked with blood. He made a quick inspection to find where the bullet had torn the pastern muscle. Petrolle was amazed that the animal had been able to run so far so fast without showing any sign of the injury until the last few miles.

'I'd really like to take time to patch you up, or get you down to Los Robles to the vet, old pard,' he said with genuine feeling. 'But a man only has so much luck in him and I've got the powerful feeling I've emptied out my supply.' He patted the mustang's muzzle. '*Muchos gracias*, pal, and like they say down here, *hasta la vista.*'

Moments later he was scaling the cliff, clambering up with the desperate agility of a startled mountain goat as hoofbeats rumbled nearer.

By the time the posse came storming up to Crystal Cliff there was no sign of either man or horse.

Marshal Matt Gant swaggered into the cell where the slender figure lay on a narrow bunk with a sheet drawn up to his chest, the room smelling of laudanum and whiskey.

The prisoner-patient was attended by a nurse in white, while two ugly deputies packing enough artillery to fuel a smallish Sonoran revolution filled corner chairs.

A big burly man with a handlebar moustache and a spuriously cheerful manner, the marshal nodded all around then straddled a chair and put on a big grin.

'So you're Cody Quinn? I gotta say you are the sorriest

piece of shit I ever did see.'

Quinn was weak as a kitten due to cracked ribs and other injuries sustained when a bullet fired at point-blank range had hammered his Colt .45 into him, his condition only mildly assisted by the fairly basic nursing administered here in the closed-off back cell of the building known as the Rimfire Jail. Only his blue eyes showed any sign of strength as the husky newcomer stared down on him like a scientist studying some new kind of bug. Jailer Graff Turnbull appeared and peered over the marshal's shoulder.

Nobody spoke but that did not bother the lawman who was here on a mission. The Rock Creek Bank's missing twenty thousand was uppermost in his thoughts.

While newspapers and front-porch sages might well have been in a lather of excitement concerning the capture of the region's boy-terror, from the law's point of view they merely had succeeded in snaring an outlaw whose sole value alive to them was the information he possessed concerning the proceeds of what had been by far his most ambitious and successful crime ever.

Quinn had to be encouraged to divulge the whereabouts of the loot after which he could be smartly tried and hanged, although there was a strong body of opinion that sickbed-to-gibbet might seem a tad inappropriate without at least a stop-over at a courthouse to go through the motions of a trial at least.

The marshal stopped grinning.

'All right, scumboy, where is it?'

No response.

Gant reached down and jammed a big thumb down upon the bandages strapped to the boy's bruise-blackened chest. He pressed hard. Beads of sweat sprang from

Quinn's brow but not a sound passed his lips.

'Hmm,' grunted Gant, as he watched fresh blood seep through the clean linen. 'This could take longer than I figured.'

'The miserable little bastard won't say nothin', Marshal,' complained fleshy, sweating Turnbull, cradling his sawed-off. 'And I gotta tell you he don't seem to feel pain neither. We was short on ether when the doc strapped up them ribs of his'n and tended to his head split there, but he never even squawked then. Mebbe it's true what they say. You know: no brains no feelin's?'

'He'll feel and he'll talk,' replied Gant, shrugging out of his jacket and rolling up his sleeves. 'Never had a failure yet.'

The old general store which now comprised Rimfire Jail was the largest building in town. Constructed of adobe brick and covered with smooth stucco, it was two storey's tall and stood on the east side of Rimfire's main street near the southern limits of that sun-baked town.

This had started out as a store serving a wide area but, with the death of the owner, had been transformed into a courthouse which at the periodical sessions of court became a scene of bustling activity, its rooms filled with lawyers and clerks and the corridors crowded with litigants from all over the wide country. But in the long intervals between, its upper floor held offenders of one breed or another, of which the youngster quartered in the cell directly above the courtroom was by far the most notorious to date.

It was not so much what Quinn did as the way he did it that had made his name a household word, and one-street Rimfire had never been more a focal point of interest than it had been since he was shipped here more dead than alive following a fifty-mile journey in a jolting prison wagon over some of the roughest trails in New Mexico.

Yet he had not complained then nor did so now as Gant went to work on his injuries again, this time with his knuckles.

'Just think of old folks eaten up with tumours and such-like where the pain would lift your scalp off, only they can't do nothing about it, Quinn. Imagine if they were lucky like you and could make it stop just by hollering, "Stop! I'll tell you where the lousy money is hid." You are a lucky man but you just don't know it.'

He bore down hard. Quinn's eyes were closed.

The turnkey breathed hoarsely, 'Hey, mebbe you kilt him, Marshal. Are you supposed to do that?'

'Of course he isn't dead,' snapped the lawman, but leaned closer over Quinn just to make sure.

Quinn's elbow whipped up and smashed into Gant's mouth, mashing lips and snapping off a tooth. Blood spattered and Gant lurched to his feet, hand to his face, white with pain and shock.

The prisoner was grinning.

In a flash, Gant's gun filled his fist and he rammed the muzzle into the outlaw's throat, finger whitening on the trigger.

'No, sir!' Turnbull yelled, seizing his gun arm. 'The chief marshal's orders, remember? Ain't nothin' fatal to happen to him until he spills his guts on the money.'

Slowly the craziness ebbed from Gant's bloodied face. He stepped back from the bunk, breathing hard. Quinn was feigning sleep.

'By God and by Judas you will pay for that you, stinking little scumsucker!' he hissed venomously, the words indis-

55

tinct due to the damage to his mouth. He shoved the gun away. Then, 'Well, don't just stand there, man, get me to your lousy doctor.'

'Sure, sure, Marshal,' Turnbull said, getting the cell door. But as the big man strode out, he muttered under his breath with some satisfaction, 'Told you he was a tough one.'

As he followed the injured man out he thought he heard a snigger from behind.

CHAPTER 4

SOUTHERN LADY

'Honey,' Mary Reece said reasonably, 'you just can't, and you know it.'

'Can't what?' he quipped. 'Take you to the summer ball tonight?'

'You know what I mean, Mitchell.'

He always knew exactly what she meant when she used that tone. She meant, 'Mitchell Reece, you are going to listen to your wife and not run off horse-hunting or some such foolishness.' Or something along similar lines. He was sober as he set down his coffee mug and picked up his hat from the kitchen dresser.

'I didn't say I would go all the way back to Alameda just on account it seems the stud's been lost again, Mary.'

'You were thinking it.'

'OK, so maybe I was. But—'

She came to him and rested her hands on his shoulders, looking up into his sunbronzed face.

'Honey, if we are meant to get Lobo back one day, then we will. But Heavens, this is the busiest part of the summer

57

and we just can't afford to have you go off again like some wandering—'

'I know, I know,' he cut in. Then he grinned. 'Anyway, he could be anywhere by now since the sheriff was killed.' He shook his head as Mary followed him out on to the back porch. 'That hammerhead has sure got to lead an adventurous life since we caught him. Wonder if he misses us?'

She squeezed his arm.

'That's the silliest question you've ever asked, Mitch. He loves you. I'd say just about as much as you love him, you old bronc stomper. Now are you going to do some honest work and let me get to mine, or not?'

He kissed her quickly and went off along the pathway to the side gate where Regal Harkeef was waiting with aristocratic dignity, swung up and kicked away across the ranch-yard under the early sun.

Summer ruled the Range.

On Mustang Ranch the chuckwagon cook, back from the roundup, was using strong solutions of lye soap to scrub out his wagon-boxes. The green of the draws was browning over some now as the summer died but the hardy buffalo grass was holding out well enough beyond the meadows where the plains reached all the way across to the Shattuck Range.

Fillies and colts with new brands burnt into silky hides jumped about in the corrals or stood in full rig tied to posts, growing accustomed to the new feel of saddles on their backs and spade bits in their young mouths.

The ramrod loped across from the sump as Mitch cleared the home acres, a spare, strong-shouldered man of thirty, reliable as the sunrise.

'Thinking of heading out Dry Creek way to look for that

yellow mare that gave us the slip today, if that's OK by you, boss.'

'Sure. Take Slim and Darby with you. I'm making a check on the water.'

There was ample water in the ground that year, thanks to good winter rains. The brown earth which, to a city man appeared so parched and empty, was now providing good service for the people who put their trust in it. Mustang Ranch's Arabs and mustangs would survive this summer well enough, so Mitch Reece was convinced by late afternoon when he turned Reg's head for home. So he got to thinking about the ball.

It was the social event of the season, or at least had been before disaster struck, and he realized he wanted to go.

They got to the function early, and looking around the hall in Rimfire with a glass in his hand and Mary looking quite lovely by his side, Mitch could see that the town was putting on a brave face while not throwing itself into the event with its customary full gusto.

Rimfire was still hurting and had been ever since some evil wind blew a youthful desperado their way one bitter spring night to clean out the vaults of the Rock Creek Bank thoroughly right down to the last white dime.

The bank had remained boarded up ever since that day up to the present. It had gone out of business along with a long list of citizens, country folk and others who'd lost everything they had.

The manhunt for Cody Quinn which had followed the robbery had been the biggest and most intense Esmeralda County ever saw, with lawmen and bounty hunters arriving from as far off as Santa Fe, El Paso and Lubbock to join in the manhunt for a 22-year-old hellion with twenty thousand in cash strapped to a stolen mustang stud.

Mitch would have joined the posses but had been laid low by a fever. But this gave added impetus to the effort and energy he'd put into the days and weeks of trailing he and his crew had done up in the high country of the Range later.

By that time a month had passed without one confirmed sighting of the bandit nor news that he'd been found lying dead someplace, victim of the fusillade of lead which had followed him out of town that night of the robbery.

This latter theory gained wide acceptance over the months that followed until even Quinn's admirers grudgingly conceded that he must be dead; that wild Cody could not possibly lie low and stay out of the warming glare of the limelight for so long.

Then just ten days ago he'd reappeared up at the stage station as large as life and eventually got to steal back his horse from the sheriff only to wind up half crippled, captured and then had been instantly 'disappeared' by the law. And still no sign of that canvas sack with the legend ROCK CREEK BANK stencilled on its side.

Following the bandit's capture, Rimfire had naturally expected its money would be recovered. That hope had long since faded. Rimfire would take years to recover, if it ever did. And how could any town bearing such a burden get to kick up its heels the way it had done on the good old days?

It seemed to Mitch Reece it might be up to him and Mary to liven things up.

He went up to the dais where the County Cowboy Banjo Band was tuning up for yet another staid waltz tune, insisted instead they deliver 'Turkey In The Straw' at full volume and cannonball tempo.

At first the Reeces were the only ones up. But they appeared to be having such a fine time that in dribs and drabs, some radiating gloomy reluctance, other couples joined them until the town hall was fairly rocking, which it continued to do until three in the morning when the band collapsed from exhaustion and it seemed unanimous that this Summer Ball might well have been the best on record. Mitch had noticed the pretty dark-haired girl dancing with the Simmonds boy earlier, smiled amiably when she approached him as he was pouring punch.

'Mr Reece, I'm Carrie Clarke, from Rimfire.'

'Mitch is the name. How are you, Carrie?'

'Oh, I'm fine. I was wondering if you might have any news on Cody?'

He showed his surprise. 'Cody? You mean—'

'Yes. I met him at the stage station in the hills some time ago, and I've been hearing all sorts of stories and rumours. . . . Do you know if he is all right?'

'Well, he is in a great deal of trouble and is being held in custody here at Rimfire—'

'Do you think they might allow me to visit him?'

He caught his wife glancing his way.

'Well, you might try it, Carrie, although I guess I wouldn't advise it.'

'Everyone hates him, don't they. . . .' she said distantly and wandered away, leaving him to carry the drinks back and explain to his wife who the pretty girl had been.

Driving home under a starry sky with Mary's head on his shoulder, Mitch had forgotten the incident and instead was reflecting on how he'd set out to do something positive to help his friends and neighbours lighten their burden that night, and in doing so had succeeded in doing the same for himself.

He realized he'd been carrying a load of guilt ever since Lobo went missing, for it was he who'd taken the stud from its wild home initially, spent an unconscionably long and bruising time accustoming the animal to captivity, bridle and saddle, and in the process had grown to love the ugly critter while winning its trust in return.

Then simply because Lobo happened to be penned up in his corral that night and not dozing atop some lofty bluff high in the Range with a midnight wind flowing through his ragged mane as he might have otherwise been, he had been stolen by somebody who probably treated him badly and never gave him a good currying, as Reece had done every single day.

Now he realized he'd been too hard on himself, and this in turn had affected those around him. From now on he would accept Lobo's fate like a man.

But that very night, in his dreams, he found himself astride the maverick broomtail. They were crossing Silverado Plateau at a flat gallop, faster, wilder and freer than anything Shattuck Range had ever seen before, running endlessly for the pure joy of it, man, horse and night all one and immortal – at least in dreams.

Even as they drove into the horse yard before the battered old house, Petrolle wasn't sure how it had all happened. They'd met by prearrangement, she had impressed him even more than before, and when she got to tell him about her father and his bullying and brutality, they'd come to a decision.

She had goods, clothing and a little money secretly saved back at the isolated farmhouse. They would go to collect them then head on south across the border and get married where the Territory law couldn't come after him over the Venture killing.

Petrolle sensed that the way he was living he'd better settle down before his past or his sins caught up with him.

The old man's jaw dropped when they arrived in the trap hauled by Lobo. He somehow held his temper while Petrolle unharnessed the mustang to water and grain him, but then his daughter began collecting her things. He started in fussing instantly. In a quiet sort of way – for him – Petrolle told him to hush up and quit annoying people.

A reasonable man might have taken the warning, considering it came from a man who radiated danger as Petrolle did. And for a while it seemed that was what he was doing, sitting on his porch rocker and muttering under his breath as he watched them begin to load up the buckboard.

It was not until his daughter emerged from the house toting the bird in the cage that the farmer jumped to his feet, ran down the rickety steps after her, red in the face with rage.

'Hetty's my bird, you thievin' harlot!' he howled. 'Gimme that cage.'

They struggled and he hauled off and hit her across the face – not for the first time. As she fell to ground, Petrolle dropped what he was carrying and started back with a curse.

Next instant he found himself looking down the barrel of a .38.

'Back up—' the angry father began, but got no further. In the space of a heartbeat Petrolle reverted to type, whipped out his Remington .44 and fired. A wild flurry of shots ensued. Mortally hit, the old man fell backwards, his gun exploding as he struck ground. Petrolle made a strange sound in his throat, took one step forward then fell face down in the yard with a bullet lodged in his heart.

The woman rushed to his side and cradled him in her arms, not looking up until the stutter of hoofs alerted her. Wild-eyed and favouring a foreleg where a wild shot had struck, the mustang stallion was gone in seconds, running with a bad limp now but still running as only a mustang could.

She was alone, father dead – wonderful! Lover dead – awful!

But she was a woman who had only known the hard way since birth, and was strong and resilient inside. Eventually she covered the bodies and went inside to make herself a strong cup of coffee.

It could be worse, she reflected.

She had the house, everything in it, eleven cows and two work-horses. She'd always known where her father hid his billfold. She went to get it and after counting the contents actually managed a smile on the way back home. She wondered if a horse with a bad leg might be able to make the twenty miles to the nearest ranch or town.

'Lottie!' Grace Bowdre called from the front room, collecting her gloves from the bureau. 'Are you coming or do I have to go driving alone and likely get taken by Apaches or something?'

'Coming, Mom.'

'You said that five minutes ago and five before—' the woman began, then broke off sharply. She hated it whenever she caught herself acting or sounding like one of those whining, ever-complaining mothers for whom motherhood seemed like the burdens of Hercules. In truth, the handsome widow of wealthy Manuel Bowdre, commission agent of Los Robles, detested the very idea of being thought of as average in any respect, not just where parenting was concerned.

So, biting her lip and telling herself to be patient, she went out front as the yard man appeared around the corner leading the buggy and the black mare.

'Good morning, Albert. Is Missy in good fettle this morning?'

'For her, pretty good, Lady Grace,' the man replied, patting the mare's glossy neck. She had always been called Lady ever since her husband brought her back to town as his bride a dozen years ago, and there was certainly something aristocratic about her style, in the way she did things, even in the way she flouted convention.

They would never understand her passion for driving here in conservative Crystal Cliffs on the fringe of the arid plains. By and large, there were two types of women in Los Robles, respectable and fallen, and anyone here could tell you to which category any particular female belonged without even having to think about it.

But any woman who dressed in the latest fashion, stepped out with any man she cared to, and spent half her time careering around the wild country in a buggy, sometimes in company but just as often all alone, just didn't fit comfortably into either classification.

Which was just how Lady Grace Bowdre liked it.

She might be a 35-year-old widow woman who was expected to live and act in a certain way, but some days she awoke feeling no more than twenty and she was damned if she would allow herself to become a prisoner of her home or her town while she still had her strength, her horses to which she was devoted, her buggy and her beloved landscape to wander at will.

Her daughter came bouncing out of the house with

pigtails flying and they were off, making their way along the main street past the stores and telegraph office, dust billowing, the mare prancing and respectable ladyfolks 'tsk-tsking' disapprovingly even though what they were seeing had been a common sight for years now.

'Where to today, Mom?'

Lottie was bright and bubbly and considered flying around the backtrails and byways of the county with her horse-loving mother infinitely preferable to school.

Grace pointed with a black kid-gloved finger at the town's nearest landmark, the glittering face of Crystal Cliffs.

'We haven't been up there in quite a time, honey. We might stop by at Rancho Amigo for lunch, or then again we might keep going all the way to the canyon, who can tell?'

As events evolved however, the travellers had covered less than ten miles before Lottie tapped her mother on the arm and pointed off to their left where two Joshua trees stood praying to the sun god by a gullywash, and said, 'Something over there moving, Mom. You don't think it might be Apaches, do you?'

Although there had not been a genuine Apache incident over the past decade here in Laporte County, they were never too far from the minds of people when out on the trails.

Lady Grace reined in to stare. Something was moving right enough but she couldn't decide what it was, although her first guess was a buffalo, possibly an injured one.

'The buffalos don't come down this far any more, Mom, you know that. I think it's a horse. Let's go see.'

The girl was right. It was a mustang lying at rest with a

bullet gash in a foreleg. The animal had lost a lot of blood and was obviously exhausted and very weak, yet the measured way it turned its large hammerhead on the short neck to study the pair was impressive even if its appearance was not.

'It's only some old wild thing, Mom. There's nothing we can do for it.'

But Lady Grace was stepping down from her rig and taking her canteen with her. She stared at the horse and it stared right back in a way that was knowing, calm and proud. She knew if the horse was left here it would surely die, was convinced he knew it too, even though his manner was proud.

'My, but isn't he something special!' Grace enthused, and went to work. It took an hour to get Lobo on his feet, after feeding him water and some corn they'd brought along for the mare.

Grace ripped up her petticoat to strap up the freshly cleansed wound, then insisted on leading the horse afoot while her daughter drove all the ten miles back to Los Robles, following the telegraph lines.

The town thought Lady Grace had finally gone round the bend when she secured the daily services of the veterinarian to tend this arrogant, injured bronco. But she persisted and within a week the stud was to be seen in the Bowdre horseyards prancing up and down and showing all the signs of a full recovery.

A week after that, disapproving matrons and puzzled storekeepers were treated to the sight of Lady Grace wheeling by in her buggy drawn, not by a glossy mare or handsome bay gelding, but rather by an unshod dun cayuse with yellow mane and tail which no amount of grooming could help look respectable – unless of course you really knew your horseflesh.

Lady Grace insisted it was the finest running horse she'd ever seen. She named him Lucky, and from that day on was not seen out on the trails with any other horse between the buggy shafts.

That midsummer's day up on the plateau three years before had been as hot as any Mitch Reece remembered.

Had he heard 'it' or was it just imagination working overtime that caused him to think he could sense the faintest of low rumblings in hazy distances, a sound like a single train almost out of earshot ., or of many hard hoofs pounding the earth . . . pounding, pounding, pounding. . . . He turned his head idly.

Chenko and Bender stood by their mounts and remounts smoking cigarettes and looking bored. They'd come out here for the action and for the chance to make some real money rounding up some wild broncs, looping them with their riatas and taking them back to Mustang Ranch for breaking.

Mitch had an order for some wild ones from a travelling Wild West show. That was his excuse for being up here. To make money. But Mary, perceptive and wise as ever, insisted that the real reason was his ongoing affection for the wild horses rather than his finding something special for this latest Barnum and Bailey of the West. Most likely she was right; she usually was about anything important.

'Hey, Mitch,' called Bender, a Mustang hand of several years, solid and dependable. 'Why don't we ride across to Maverick Point and take a look-see? I cut some sign over that way a couple of weeks back.'

'We sure ain't gonna make any money up here,' supported lantern-jawed Chenko, a wild horse hunter from up Roswell way whom Mitch had not worked with before. He made a sweeping gesture. 'Look, no dust, no sign, nothin' but this stinkin' sun boilin' a man's brains. I say let's hightail.'

He didn't like Chenko. The man was too rough and arrogant to suit. Yet he rode well, an essential in this kind of work, and he looked tough enough for the job too.

'We're staying put,' he said bluntly.

Bender just shrugged but Chenko glared and came across from the horses with his high-shouldered, loose-jointed walk.

'I signed on to hunt broomtails, Reece, and—'

'That's Mitch or Mr Reece.'

Twin spots of color showed on the horseman's gaunt cheekbones.

'All right – Mister Reece. But you signed me up to help you run in some broncs, so much per head, and I'm earnin' zero sittin' up here on this mesa like a turkey buzzard. This plain don't suit.'

'Nobody's holding you here.'

'You tellin' me to shove off?'

'I'm telling you to—' Mitch broke off. There it was again. Clearer this time. A distant drumroll of sound coming in from the north. And now as he stared in that direction, the dust that Chenko had looked for in vain was suddenly visible, a rising cloud of the stuff, butter-coloured in slanting sunlight, climbing above the bluffs now, raised by scores of hoofs slamming the earth in the drumbeat of freedom.

And now as all three men stood staring towards the bluffs they swept into sight, hoofs glinting, uncombed tails flying like sails in the wind.

The wild ones, heading their way!

'It's still your choice,' Mitch snapped at Chenko as he trotted for the appaloosa. 'Stay or go, all the same to me,' he said, now slapping his thigh and sporting a huge grin as he ran towards his stringers.

'If it's all the same to you I'll be stayin' with you, boss man. They told me you could sniff these critters out and, doggone, they are right. Let's git dustin'.'

The herd was making for the canyon east of the mesa and within moments the three riders were sliding their horses down the steep slope, heading east. They had not been sighted yet, and the herd kept coming, dozens of them down from the Range, running for a purpose or simply for the sheer joy of it – it was impossible to tell.

Wild and savage as any wolf or bear, these were the descendants of the wonderful Barbs from Spain brought to the New World by the conquistadors three centuries ago.

The breed had been large once but the generations that had run wild had been pared down to bare essentials by drought, combat, the ferocious south-western winters and the eternal struggle to stay alive in a hostile land. Now they were smallish with big heads and leather-lean legs tapering down to rock-hard hoofs. Even so, they could still be caught. But only by men who knew them and understood their ways. Men like Mitch Reece, and yes, Chenko from Roswell.

The mob shrieked with anger and picked up their pace when two horsemen burst from the shadows of a giant black boulder, swinging lariats and hooting and hollering.

Soon the fleet-footed quarry had increased their lead, yet the dark blobs of the two chasers clung to their dust like seed burrs.

Mitch and Bender raced side by side with bandannas

drawn up over their noses, allowing the mob to draw away for a time, holding their mounts to a gallop but refusing to flog them into greater speed.

This was not a test of speed but of stamina.

Five hours later they were still riding, still within sight of the seemingly tireless herd. In that time they had covered many miles, but the mob was already displaying the weakness, not in their physical stamina or spirit but in their instincts which were based on habit. Right now, after running such a great distance, they were once again approaching the mesa from the north as they had done before. This was their current range and they chose to stick to it, a potentially fatal mistake when there were hunters like Reece about who figured they would do just that.

By the time the racing bunch drew abreast of the mesa, the pursuing riders and their pards were all played out. But Chenko had spent the time relaxing in the cool shade, occasionally getting up to give his sorrel water and a rub down. And as Mitch and Bender finally quit the chase and swung out of the drag dust towards Black Boulder, Chenko was in his saddle and taking off after the broncos.

If the wild ones again clung to their running range, by the time they reached the mesa again they would be exhausted at last and ripe for the plucking at the hands of a refreshed Reece and Bender with their long lariats and forking mint-fresh remounts.

Hours later, the slowing horse mob reappeared but there was no sign of Chenko. The two men forked their broncs swiftly to go galloping north along the trail. This was dangerous work and there were any number of pitfalls for a chaser to fall into, particularly when riding alone.

They heard the shot when they'd been in the saddle

some thirty minutes; it came from beyond Buzzard Mesa where a tense drama was being played out between horse and man.

The horse was the dun-coloured stud with the wild mane and tail, the man was Chenko the rugged horse-hunter from Roswell.

The pretty mare was just the cause of it all.

The stallion was leading the mob as it had been throughout that mighty run, when above the pounding of the hoofbeats echoing back from Buzzard Mesa, he heard it. The high, whinnying cry for help from somewhere in the rear.

Instantly the stud slowed its pace, eyes rolling whitely as it stared back through dust and distorting heat haze, searching firstly for the solitary rider who had been hammering after them for so long, secondly for the source of that cry for help.

He sighted the mare first. It had come down a half mile behind, injuring a foreleg on a loose stone. It had struggled to its feet to hobble on but proved no match for the rider, who'd tossed his rope over its head, now was dragging it after him as though deaf to the animal's cries of pain.

Chenko's purpose was to take the injured mare – one of the finest horses in the bunch – as far as Black Boulder to rejoin Reece and Bender; he was certain it would fetch top dollar in Roswell.

The dun watched from a shaly knoll. It stood motionless, head raised, ears pointed forwards, dark eyes flicking yellow at the corners. Chenko's eyes widened when he saw the stallion, one of the largest and most probably the finest animal in the whole mob. It ran better than any horse he'd ever seen, so well in fact that the man held no real hope of snagging it when they went for the exhausted mob at the boulder. It would surely still prove too fast, too tough and too crafty to be caught, as befitted that status and stamina of the leader of a mob this size.

To see it closer than it had been all day, and motionless, sent a shiver down the horse-hunter's spine. 'You bastard. . . .' he began admiringly, but broke off when the mare whinnied again, and the stud went up on its hind legs, pawing at the air and blowing warningly through a dusty muzzle.

Instantly Chenko understood. The stud wanted to play hero. Frighten the big bad horse-hunter off and doubtless help his injured sweetheart make it into the hills to recover.

The hell he would!

Chenko was far more interested in the stud than the mare now as he wound in his rope, dragging his limping catch closer until it was within reach of a rope's end.

Deliberately, viciously, he cut the mare across the face with the hard rope, almost bringing it to its knees.

'C'mon, hero!' he taunted as he swung the rope again. 'Come and do your stuff if you reckon you're up to it. Heeyahhh!' he roared, and now drove his lathered mount into the mare knocking it to the ground. It struggled to rise but, reaching from the saddle, Chenko kicked it to the side of the jaw, stunning it and causing the handsome head to drop.

The dun whistled shrilly and the mare replied with a sound almost too weak to be heard.

The dun advanced as Chenko licked his lips and readied his riata. Rock-hard hoofs clattered and now the dun was beginning to circle him, snorting, arching its breedy neck.

'She's all yours, lover boy. All you gotta do is come take her off of me. Shouldn't be no big thing for an ugly piece of horse-shit like you. What are you waitin' for?'

But the dun kept circling, the diameter of the circle narrowing with each turn. Slowly turning his mount to keep facing the wild horse, Chenko was absorbed and intent as a man could be yet still missed the implication of the sudden sharp snort of sound which was the only warning the stallion gave before it suddenly launched itself at him in a huge, panther-like spring which saw it cover some twenty feet to go completely beneath the weak, wild play of the lasso that the rider made both too slow and too late.

Next instant Chenko was flying through the air as his terrified mount was slammed sideways by the impact of an equine chest that hit like a pile-driver. Rolling in rocks and dust with blood running from his mouth, the man could not believe any of it. His gun was gone and he'd let go of the rope's end looped around his saddle horn. As he came up on one knee he saw the mare on its feet, the stud nudging it forward, trying to urge it into a trot.

Chenko went loco.

Spotting his pistol lying in the dust, he flung himself upon it, rolled once and came up shooting.

He got just one shot away before the piece jammed. But it was enough. The stallion screamed and went down and Chenko snatched his boot rifle from his horse and attacked the stallion's head, bringing down big brutal blows in his fury, some glancing off head and neck but others connecting solidly.

Blood streamed from the horse's head, and the man was systematically beating it to death when two riders came surging up through the choking dust and leapt to the ground.

In that moment as Reece stared into the eyes of the horse that was destined to play so important a part in his life, he saw rage, defiance and hatred, yet at the same time sensed some kind of plea reaching out to him by one of earth's creatures to another.

Chenko's face was ugly as he raised the rifle butt to swing again, and Reece came out and used a charging shoulder before giving it a second thought.

Chenko went over, the rifle clattering away on the pebbles. The blood-streaked mustang struggled to rise but the bullet had taken it in the shoulder, causing the foreleg to collapse.

As Bender took charge of the animal, Chenko erupted to his feet, raging. 'You uppity son of a bitch, Reece! What the hell do you think you're doin'?'

'Keep away from that horse,' Mitch said quietly, chest heaving. 'That's not the way we hunt here, mister.'

'Don't tell me my business, mister. Anyway, he's my catch and I'll do what I please with the bastard. Git out of the way—'

'No bronc belongs to any man till he's put a rope on him.' Mitch indicated Bender. 'That's a Mustang Ranch animal.'

Mitch was expecting it.

He swayed out of reach of a whistling punch then ripped a jab to Chenko's ribs, lifting the bigger man off his feet. As Chenko gasped and staggered he stopped a hook to the cheekbone and an uppercut to the side of the jaw. Raging mad, he retaliated with a haymaker that had Mitch walking backwards. Chenko dropped his head and charged, arms flailing, dribbling blood and curses. Mitch calmly measured the man off and belted him to the mouth, stopping him in his tracks. Chenko was a lopped tree looking for someplace to fall. Mitch kicked his legs from beneath him and he hit dirt face first.

Bender was impressed.

'Guess he had that coming, Mitch.'

'No guess about it,' Mitch panted. 'Is that horse going to live?'

'Might be better off to put it put of its misery.'

It looked that way. And maybe Mitch Reece might have pulled his shooter right then and there, but for the look. It was as if the blood-streaked stallion's look he gave Reece, as he loomed above him again, had a damn-you-to-hell defiance in the depths of his wild eyes, yet there was something else, some quality of acknowledgement of what had taken place combined with a silent plea. 'Don't kill me, I don't want to die on such a fine day.'

And he didn't.

That had all happened three years back, almost to the day. Mitch was lost in the past as he came in off the meadows to the home acres but came jolting back to the here and now when he realized he had vistors. Important visitors.

CHAPTER 5

CAGED AND DANGEROUS

They'd shifted the prisoner from his pokey ground-floor cell up to the courtroom, a big stark room that occupied the entire western side of the second storey and was lighted by six windows, two in front overlooking the street, two at the back and two in the east wall.

Beyond the judge's bench at the rear of the chamber, raised on a low dais, with the jury box opposite and the railed-off enclosure where the clerk and other court officials had their desks, was a hallway which gave on to a roofed-over, second-storey porch along the front of the building, leading to a stairway adjacent to a heavy oaken door.

This door was always kept padlocked for it was the armoury where rifles and revolvers and suchlike were stored for emergency use by the sheriff's posses from time to time.

They had been guarding bad Cody day and night, and

now that he was up and about, they had him linked by a ten-foot length of ankle chain linked to a heavy steel ring bolt set in the stone wall directly beneath a sombre and unsmiling picture of the President.

The medico was puzzled but impressed as he completed his examination of the most infamous prisoner ever to come under his charge.

'Beats all,' he told Turnbull, who occupied the judge's handsome big chair, looking like a hog lolling on a silken bed.

'A week ago I was pretty sure he might croak, but look at him now. Beat up plenty, but sound as a bell. How do you do it, son?'

'Clean living,' came the laconic response from the prisoner. 'What else?'

Quinn had one eye shut, a swollen top lip and any number of cuts and abrasions. The medico had re-taped his forehead which had been deeply gashed during his capture, and had finally stopped bandaging the ribs which were healing well now. Most of the other injuries were of a recent and suspicious origin.

'I'm puzzled some, sonny. If you know where the bank money is hid why not tell them before they kill you?'

'That'll be enough, Doc,' Turnbull called. 'You've done your job, now beat it.'

'Shove it, Graff,' the man replied. 'The day I take orders from any turnkey is the day I'll know I'm too blamed old for this job.'

'You are too old,' the turnkey sulked. 'You'd be out on your ass if there was another sawbones in fifty miles.'

'Shortage of medicos is the curse of the West, ain't you heard?' The doctor smirked maliciously. 'Although, come to think on it, how would you hear, Graff Turnbull? You

78

don't read the papers, do you? Why is that now?'

'I'm warnin' you', croaker—'

'He can't read,' weighed in Quinn, reaching for his tobacco. 'Can you believe that, Doc? Here I am, Cody Quinn the famous badman kept all hogtied and helpless by a poor lonesome wife-left fella who can't even read or write his own John Henry. Oh, the shame of it all.'

Hoofbeats drifted up from the street. The turnkey heaved himself out of his chair and slouched to a window. Just some plainsmen coming in for the day. He turned back to the room, hitching the gun-belt that sagged beneath his drum gut. 'You still here, Doc?'

The doctor closed his black bag with a snap and made his way to the hallway entrance, where he halted, washed-out grey eyes quizzical behind pince-nez. 'Who's been beating up on him, turnkey? You or the marshal?'

'Nobody is who. You're imaginin' things.'

'It'll go on my report that he's getting beaten up by the day, in my professional opinion. Should he cash in, you will share responsibility, Turnbull.'

The turnkey crossed the room with his heavy, dragging step. He was a youngish man aged by overweight. He had three chins, a pendulous underlip and managed to appear menacing, unsure and smug all at once.

'This is Rimfire, Doc. Not Roswell or Alamogordo. There ain't nobody for you to go tale-tellin' to hereabouts, which is how it should be. Me and my sawed-off here is the law here right now, and that geezer in the corner yonder is just a biggety little prick we're gonna hang sooner or later as sure as God made little green apples. That's what we want and what the Territory wants. So who's gonna listen to anythin' any broken-down has-been like you might say? Go get yourself a slug, Doc. Get yourself drunk and leave us to tend to jokers who'd carve up the likes of you long, wide and deep, given half a chance. Don't waste no tears on this one.'

'It's the marshal, isn't it?' the man said stubbornly. 'He's torturing the prisoner to force him tell him where that money is hid.'

'You ain't still here, are you?'

'I've got news for you,' the doctor offered as a parting shot. 'That one won't crack. I've seen too many men facing sickness, pain, death or execution in my time not to be able to size them up. This man might be a mad dog but he's a dog that's all gristle and grit, just the opposite of you!'

A soft chuckle caused the turnkey to whirl.

The prisoner was leaning against the whitewashed wall blowing smoke from his nostrils in twin white jets.

'He's right, turnkey. He's got you tabbed neat and straight. No balls is your big handicap. You just know deep down inside that you're going to wake up one of these starry nights with me tapping you on the shoulder to tell you your throat's just been cut, and you are scared to hell. I don't blame you. I'd scare myself if I wasn't scare-proof by nature.'

Angry words leapt to Turnbull's lips but he bit them off. He had learned early on he couldn't win a verbal joust with his charge. The kid was as quick and lethal with the tongue as he was with a sixgun. Turnbull swung back and returned to the judge's chair, wishing he was a real judge wearing a black cap and sentencing the prisoner to swing on the gibbet right outside. Now. Today. Before lunch.

Quinn just chuckled mockingly and extended his chain to its limit in order that he might get to reach the window where he looked out on a day just as big and bright-skied as any he had ever seen.

Far out a tiny dust spiral danced upon a patch of yellow sand until it vanished amongst some cottonwoods. Cody danced with it, free and singing. Beyond the cottonwoods and the hills the great mountains rested on the horizon like blue clouds.

He sighed.

He was now staring up at the distinctive, craggy-topped outline of the Shattuck Range, home of most every breed of wild critter to be found in this quarter of the country and which, for about ten weeks straight at least, had been home to young Cody Quinn.

It was like a clean wind blowing through his mind just to think back to himself and that dun-coloured stud roaming about up there all free and safe in their hideaway while legions of red-faced possemen, hawk-eyed trailsmen and bloody-handed bounty hunters by the dozen were beating the bushes for him in the hope of nailing him, recovering the bank haul and collecting the huge reward on offer, enough to keep a man in luxury the rest of his days.

He had to smile.

Luck had been with him the night of the big robbery when he'd made it almost to Mustang Ranch on a fast-fading cayuse, there to find a broomtail with an engine in him like a locomotive just waiting to carry him up into the high country before all the massed forces of the county could roll over him, wash him up and hang him out to dry.

He'd subsequently led a charmed, if lonesome, life in the high Shattucks, but for the incident that had cost him his mustang stallion.

It was blind luck, pure and simple which led that Rimfire posse to stumble upon his camp that night. He blew three of them away but was forced to shimmy-slide away down a thousand feet of mountain slope to evade the others. He succeeded but was forced to hide out for several days, by which time Lobo was long gone, had wandered back to the plains as he was to find out later. By the time he was ready to quit the Shattucks he'd learned his horse had been found and apparently claimed by the sheriff.

But his reliable good luck had been with him when he finally decided he'd had his fill of both the high lonesome and the Crater, and made it all the way back down to the plains, first to steal back his mustang from horse-thieving Sheriff Venture then head up north for a rip-roaring reunion with old friends at Rooney Ranch.

But fate caught up with him in a rush later that same night when he ducked out to carve himself a chunk of prime smoked ham and returned to his nice airy bedroom only to be jumped by a vengeful peace officer, and came within an inch of losing his life when that .45 went off at point-blank range.

He'd actually believed he felt Death's hoary breath upon his young face as that rotten old bastard stood over him with a smoking gun and breathing hate so fierce you could smell it – but quick wits had saved him. Yet again.

Whoever would have thought that the big dinero he'd stolen would save his life that night when Venture realized he couldn't kill him for fear of losing all hope of recovering that twenty grand. And on an even brighter note, what about the poetic justice in Grandfather Venture being found cold and stiff one morning soon afterwards with his ugly old mug locked in the final grimace of violent death, with his pockets emptied and the stud gone with the wind. Again.

Then it pleased him to start tallying up all the many

people who had tried to kill him over the years, and how few of them were still alive today. Close as he could calculate, Venture would have been around number seventeen. It was on record that he had personally slain thirteen men, and the list of those who'd died hunting him or as a direct result of their efforts to bring him to book stood at somewhere between four and five. So far.

The marshal would be number eighteen. And if God was good, Turnbull would make nineteen before he was through. As his name slotted into the mind of the young watcher from the courtroom window, Marshal Matt Gant emerged from the Royal Flush saloon and diner across the way, picking his teeth and squinting against the glare coming off the street.

The prisoner's face was expressionless as he watched the big man from the marshal's office make his leisurely way across the street. Gant was twice his size and strong as an ox yet Quinn didn't fear him. He feared nobody and nothing except boredom. His innocent blue eyes flicked across at Turnbull as the man rose at the sound of boots upon the stairs.

Gant.

Pain was on its way.

Yet the outlaw knew he could take it today just as he had done every day since his arrival. Gant had a mission. But likewise so did Quinn. His was to stay alive until he got the chance to splatter Gant's blood and entrails from one end of this skinny main stem to the other, then hightail it back into those pretty blue mountains and the big dinero in its secret cache.

Gant adapted a different approach today. Having tried extreme brutality without getting to first base, the marshal, drawing up a chair and calmly lighting up a

cheroot, was determined to rely on logic and persuasive-
ness instead.

'Let's go over it again, kid. From page one. You rob the
bank – no question about that. You were lucky there,
because the bank is holding extra dinero overnight, due
to a government payroll due to be transported from
Rimfire to Roswell next day. So, you get rich and lucky that
day. But people are yelling for your balls before you make
it to Reece's ranch on an ailing horse, snatch another and
disappear into the Range with your horse and your cash
for goddamn near three months. You're with me up to
that stage of the game, are you, boy?'

Cody leaned lazily against his wall. 'Suck snake eggs,
dung-eater.'

Gant coloured but maintained his relaxed pose and
dignified tone.

'What we need to know, Cody, what we must know, is
did you bust out of the Range with your booty, or did you
leave the bank money stashed up in the high country or
maybe someplace else? Surely that's not too much to ask?
From one reasonable man to another? Huh?'

The lawman was faking patience and sweet reasonable-
ness. Too bad it was all falling on deaf ears.

'Don't you mean: from one wall-eyed horse's ass – you –
to the richest, luckiest outlaw in New Mexico – me –
Marshal?'

Quinn was sprawled unconscious on the floor by the
time Gant stamped from the courthouse sector a short
time later. The turnkey, who was growing tired of all this
heavy security and weighty responsibility, was hoping the
squirt might croak it this time even as he looked around
for somebody to send out for the doctor again.

But he didn't.

Cody was not ready to die yet. He had too much getting square to take care of. And after that, some real living to put in. Just himself, a good horse and twenty thousand beautiful dollars.

Lobo halted in the shafts, head hanging, legs widespread and dripping sweat. She hated doing it, but Lady Grace swung the buggy whip to cut the stud across the haunches, her face grimacing with regret as the animal flinched and lurched. 'Please, Lucky, you must, you must,' she cried. 'I think she is unconscious now . . . do try to understand. Go, go!'

The mustang's jaw hung open and a trickle of blood ran from the gaping mouth. It was hardly in any condition to walk, much less run. Of course it did not understand. Only knew the woman wanted him to keep running even though he had already run too far . . . that the woman had been kind to him . . . that he was born to run. . . .

He lurched forward again and the buggy jounced after him over the jagged stones and deep ruts of terrain that would be difficult enough for men on horseback and totally unfit for vehicles.

And the blood and sweat coursed freely again and the girl tossed fitfully on the buggy seat semi-conscious in the blanketing heat while the woman drove, kneeling with her hair full of dust and desperation in her eyes, as she saw the land before her climbing, climbing, seemingly forever against the burning sky. The nightmare had begun in the simplest possible way. They were thirty miles south of Los Robles, as far from home as they ever went, bowling along a rough trail flanking a deep gullywash with Lobo running like greased joy and mother and daughter singing, when the rabbit appeared.

There was no telling what made it come shooting out of the brush on the right the way it did, to angle at full speed across the path of the horse, and then disappear beneath a low-hung juniper.

Yet it startled Grace so that she reflexively jerked on the reins, jerked hard enough to pull Lobo off-stride, to stumble, to fight desperately to straighten up before the off-side wheel went into the wash and buggy, horse and passengers were rolling over in a headlong crash to the bottom.

Lottie was thrown clear but landed on her stomach on a rough upthrust of stone and knocked unconscious. Lobo was up quickly but limping with severe pain from a shoulder sprain and a deeper hurt in the chest.

Only Grace was unhurt and to her went the grim responsibility of deciding what was to be done. The first thing that jumped into her mind was that the Los Robles doctor was absent in the west country attending to a childbirth. She could return to town and wire the next nearest physician, eighty miles distant at Burning River, hope to find him available and – much more unlikely – ready to take the enormous journey to Los Robles to attend her daughter.

Or else she could set out from where she now stood, staring at the rugged hill country before her, try to fight her way through to the Sundown Plains to pick up the railroad at Silver Point for the ten-mile journey to Burning River. Twenty miles of hell with an unconscious child and an injured horse. That was her option and she took it, hadn't had to take the whip to her beautiful mustang until over half the terrible journey was behind them and Lucky looked as though he might be dying on his feet.

But he kept on running through the brush and the

stones, weaving between trees and outcroppings of mesquite, slogging onwards and seemingly ever upwards over a slope which didn't seem to know how to end.

But end it did and they were weaving down with glimpses of the great plain visible from time to time as the buggy bounced and pitched and the woman struggled to hold her daughter on the seat and the dun ran without guidance and somehow managed to avoid every obstacle that might impede or stop them forever. Running. . . .

But that matchless stride was ragged now and he slowed often, tossing his head in distress, groaning from pain and exhaustion, finally beginning to stumble only when flat and treeless earth surrounded them in the long plains twilight. And Lady Grace wept for her child and what she'd been forced to do to the horse, then wept tears of relief when lights twinkled against the darkened plain ahead, the lights evolving into a scatter of unpainted buildings and a tiny rail depot before the horse went down and was unable to rise.

People came from the town and soon Lottie was being tended by a provincial nurse at the depot as they waited for the nine o'clock train to Burning River, and Charlie Gunn the vet brought the bad news to Grace.

'Hoss is done for I'm afeared, Lady. Got a busted rib and I reckon it's punctured the lung. Lord knows how much blood he's lost but I doubt he'll make it through the night.'

'You won't let him suffer, will you, Charlie?' she pleaded, as the shriek of a whistle breached the night's hush.

She didn't say any more but Charlie knew exactly what she meant. And a short time after the winking red caboose lights of the departing train faded into the darkness, the vet walked into his horse stall where they'd taken the stud, old-fashioned Dragoon Colt in his hand and wearing his spectacles, so he wouldn't miss.

Lobo lay prone on clean straw with only the eyes and heaving ribcage showing signs of life. He stared up at the man and the horse-loving vet of Silver Point just stood there staring back. Maybe Charlie Gunn was too soft-hearted to be a really good horse doctor, and he asked himself the question: why upset himself by doing something that Mother Nature was bound to take care of within the next hour or two? And though he wouldn't pretend to be able to read a horse's mind, it seemed to him that this broomtail wanted to hang on to the very last minute, just like Charlie expected to do when his time came.

He walked out and made his way to the saloon for a couple of stiff ones before heading on home. When he returned to the stables next day, he walked in then took three backwards steps in total astonishment.

The stud was looking at him over the half door of the feed stall, cheeks bulging with the grain it was munching.

A wire had reached town in the early hours with the news that Lottie Bowdre was out of danger. Charlie might have sent Lady Grace a wire in return giving her the good news on her nag. But if he did that he supposed she would expect to come collect him one day and, after all, she had turned the critter over to him to do with as he might, hadn't she?

Charlie was a good man. He'd seen the ad in the newspaper over recent weeks where a well-known horseman and rancher name of Mitch Reece was offering a reward for any information on a missing mustang stallion which fitted Lucky's description to a T.

He got off a wire and a grateful Reece showed up to

claim the mustang but was not able to persuade Charlie to take the promised reward.

'It's repayment enough just to see how happy you and that hoss are to see one another, Mr Reece,' he insisted.

There seemed to be something about this broomtail bronco that genuine horse-lovers just couldn't resist.

CHAPTER 6

CODY'S SECRET

The dignitaries from Rimfire visited Mitch Reece together on the Monday. He discussed their request with Mary and gave them his answer.

He finally reluctantly agreed to go visit Cody Quinn and question him about the cache as requested – if they still considered him the man for the job. But he wanted it made clear he didn't want Rimfire's deputation or anybody else holding out high expectations on the outcome.

'Even if it happened the way we reckon, that he stashed the cache someplace up in the Range,' he told them. 'I just don't see any good reason why he should tell me, seeing as he hasn't already spilled to the authorities. And to tell the truth I still can't quite figure why you gentlemen came to me anyway.'

'I'll give you the reasons, Mitch,' said the sober-minded mayor, dewlaps hanging over high starched collar. 'Firstly, we're dealing with a real tough *hombre* here, and I can tell you honestly there's mighty few men in this town who'd have the grit to go through with this, all things considered. But you're different. You're young, you're tough and you've always had the interests of Rimfire at heart, which made us think you might be willing to help out. Then there's the fact that Quinn stole that broomtail of yours and kept him with him all those months he went missing, so that gives you a kind of personal connection to the man, don't you see? I mean, that and the fact that both of you seem just a little bit touched in the head when it comes to that particular wild nag, if you don't mind my saying so.'

'That hellion outlaw is done for and he just might open up to someone who's got no connection with the law or politics or anything like,' cut in the big-nosed sheriff, who hated Cody Quinn something fierce but wouldn't dare go within rifle range of the badman to save himself. 'But let's be honest, Mitch, the rock-solid main reason we thought of you is that everyone likes you.'

The man grinned fatuously, giving fair warning he was about to be 'witty'. 'Why, folks say around town . . . even Mitch Reece's enemies like him.'

Mitch remained expressionless. Silent. The man sobered and tugged his waistcoat down over a swelling paunch.

'But it's true you do have the knack with folks. If anyone can talk that lousy little scut into spilling where he hid that money so we can get it back and save our town from ruin, it has to be you.'

Mitch might well be flattered although he was still far from optimistic. But as he rose from his chair to stand in the doorway to stare across his ranch, he found himself reiteratating that which he and Mary had agreed upon. It had to be at least worth a try.

The town of Rimfire had been slowly dying ever since the bank robbery. Quinn had subsequently disappeared, been arrested then beaten, starved and threatened with death but refused to divulge the whereabouts of the twenty thousand in cash. This, coupled to the fact that not a cent of that money had surfaced since the robbery, suggested strongly that it just might still be up there on the Range someplace, likely intact. If this was the case, then all Mitch felt that he would need was a small miracle that might influence the young outlaw to decide to open up to someone apart from the authorities and reveal the cache's whereabouts before they dropped him through the trap-door.

Of course, he would need to forget all about the troubles the kid had caused Lobo if he was to handle the chore properly and calmly. Otherwise he might just walk into that jail and do what he felt most like doing, namely hand him a good licking.

Lobo was full of running as Mitch Reece left Mustang Ranch behind in their dust. Halfway to Nobletown Lake the menacing weather rolled across the county line and clouds of light rain swept the earth from the starkness of an angry sky. Remote thunder crashed and rolled as jagged thrusts of lightning danced and writhed in the distance.

It rained every long mile to the high plain upon which Rimfire stood, one of those violent summer rains that could hit this part of the country this time of year, converting the prairies into quagmires that made it hard-going even for a horse as strong as the stallion.

Reece camped overnight on the edge of the plain and awoke next day to brilliant sunshine, again typical of the climatic changes of both region and season. The distant blot of colour on the sodden landscape that was Rimfire showed directly ahead.

An hour later he dropped off the horse at the livery and was now being hailed from the law office porch upon the long main stem as he made for the two-storey courthouse building on foot. The man was tall and powerfully built with a marshal's badge pinned to a barrel chest. Marshal Matt Gant, as he was about to discover, was not the easiest man to deal with.

'You want to what?' the badgeman snorted when Mitch halted him and stated his case. 'You think you can just wander in off the goddamn prairie, claim to represent someone or other then get to see this maverick son of a bitch just like that? We run a high-security jailhouse in case you don't know it, mister—'

'Reece. Mitch Reece off of Mustang Ranch over in Esmeralda County.'

'I don't care if you're . . . hey, did you say Mustang Ranch?'

'That's right.'

'Then you'd be the rancher Cody stole that hoss from on his runout from the big bank job in the summer? The mustang stallion?'

'Right.'

At least the marshal knew about Lobo, which lent Mitch some credibility. They lit cigarettes and in a calmer atmosphere he listed for Gant most of the reasons that had brought him here and exactly what he hoped to achieve by the visit.

But the marshal remained anything but optimistic. 'He

won't tell you the time of day. I'm a professional and I can tell you he's the toughest nut I've ever struck.'

'Have you got anything to lose by me talking to him?'

Thoughtful for a time, the lawman was finally obliged to respond in the negative. Then he shrugged, asked for Mitch's Colt, and invited his visitor to accompany him upstairs to the courtroom.

There, Mitch was left in the company of a hulking turnkey armed with a double-barrel sawed-off shotgun and a smiling, lithe-hipped kid who showed manifest signs of brutal treatment.

Yet Quinn proved to be cheery and cheeky when he realized who it was who'd come calling.

'If you're looking for your bronco, horseman, they wouldn't let me bring him up here for some fool reason.' He grinned and rattled his length of chain. 'Hope you don't hold it against me, that business of my sneaking on to your place that night and snatching your mustang. I was a tad, you know, kind of desperate.'

He chuckled at the recollection and glanced out his window, affording his visitor time to study him more closely.

Mitch was surprised bordering on the astonished.

Naturally there'd been pictures and sketches aplenty in the press during Quinn's widely publicized apprehension. But knowing what the man looked like in black-and-white didn't really prepare you for the flesh-and-blood reality. The press claimed he was twenty-two but he looked more like seventeen as he turned back to him. 'So, I guess you've come a long ways for nothing, huh?' It was not easy to sit opposite the outlaw with the boy's face and believe he was a bandit and cold-blooded killer. He sensed a keen intelligence in the innocent blue gaze and was astute enough to assess the litheness and latent power in the slender body. The prisoner's face and body showed signs of brutal treatment, and he guessed he mightn't have to look very far beyond the ugly-faced Turnbull to figure who might be responsible.

The prisoner stopped smiling abruptly and the blue eyes turned cold and supicious in a twinkling.

'There's no keeping secrets in this man's town,' he said flatly. 'You're here to try and pump me about the cache after old ugly-knuckles and his buddies over there have worked their fat asses off trying to loosen my tongue and got noplace. So what hope does a hick bronco-buster like you have? Zero, is what. So you can save your breath and vanish – unless of course you want to talk about my bronco. Well, he was yours, but we got to be great buddies up in the Shattucks, and I guess I always had a natural way with critters, so I reckon it'd be wise on your part to realize if he ever shows up again that him and me'll take up where we left off.'

'I'd be willing to stand both of us in front of Lobo and see which one he'd come to,' Mitch was surprised to hear himself retort.

The killer fell silent for a moment, smiling, eyes dreamy, as though he might be recalling racing through a night laced with danger on a stolen dun mustang with a leather sack containing $20,000 banknotes. But seeing behind that sunny smile and blue-eyed mask with some ease now, Mitch Reece reckoned he could detect the cold steel and the harnessed ferocity just beneath the surface.

He put his case, the other heard him out politely enough, then simply shrugged. It was as if he'd said, 'Quit wasting both our time, horseman. If you were in my boots, would you give them the satisfaction?'

By the time Turnkey Turnbull had produced a grudging mug of coffee, Mitch was beginning to understand fully how Quinn might very well have done all those things he stood accused of, acquiring a wide notoriety in the process. But the outlaw was plainly not about to do any favours for Mitch Reece, the Rock Creek Bank or anybody else on the planet. He was dead certain of that, but had hardly gotten to accept the fact that he'd failed when the outlaw suddenly winked conspirationally and surprised him again.

'What are you like at back-scratching, horseman?'

'What?'

'Well, we could scratch each other's backs on this one.'

Mitch glanced across at Turnbull who was slumped in the judge's tall chair again, sawed-off across meaty knees, staring dully at nothing.

When he turned back the prisoner was lazily gazing out from what had become something of a local feature named Cody's Window. Following the man's gaze, Mitch sighted a trio of young women standing on the opposite walk. They looked up and waved. Quinn touched his puffed lips with his fingertips and threw a mock salute. One girl grabbed another by the arm and all three giggled, despite the scowling disapproval of a passing couple in drab range rig. 'Man, oh, man! Am I fixing to have myself a wild old time when I bust out of here, horseman old pal.'

The outlaw leaned closer confidentially.

'Between me and you I just play up to all the ladyfolks to rile that big-belly turnkey yonder. He can't stand it on account nobody in a petticoat has ever looked at him sideways and never blamed will. It gets under Gant's hide too – the son of a bitch. You know, that marshal honestly reckons he's something special. But I can tell you, pilgrim, lock me and him in a dark room with no weapons any day you fancy, and when you open the door he'd be dead and I'd be laughing, just like I am now—'

He broke off abruptly, instantly sober again.

'OK, back to business. You're a cleanskin, rancher. You also seem smart enough, if I'm any judge. Ambitious too, I hope. So listen close. But first thing, you gotta believe this. I'm a dead man setting here . . . mebbe I'm so sure of that I've even made my peace with the Maker. I gave up hope of staying alive long back but I reckon I'd still do most anything I can get to breathe free air again. Hell! I'd even be ready and willing to kiss that big dinero goodbye just to live. You believe what I'm saying?'

'No.'

The killer threw his head back and laughed.

'I like you, horse-buster. And I can see now why those fat-assed old money grubbers tapped you for the job of talking me around: you're the sort of geezer folks naturally trust and—'

'Get on with it, man,' Mitch cut in. 'What are you trying to say?'

'Simple. Smuggle me in a shooter and in return I'll let you know perzackly where I hid that money you're all so het-up about. What have you got to lose? I'm nothing to you. It doesn't matter one sweet damn to you if they stretch my neck a dozen times here or if I take a boat to Rio and get a job as a towel-boy in a brothel. You're not going to sleep any different nights one way or the other. You'd be stinking rich. But you'll also be the biggest hero in the Territory, and, you know, I've a feeling you're the kind of geezer who'd fancy wearing that sort of flash hat. What do you say?'

Mitch proceeded to say plenty. But none of it was what the other wanted to hear. And yet, disappointed as he was to learn Mitch wouldn't be party to a deal, Cody Quinn took it like a man.

'No hard feelings, Reece.' He smiled, shaking hands and revealing a grip of incredible strength. 'Sure, they'll kill me now . . . but what the hell. I've been dodging the Grim Reaper all my life. But you'd better believe you won't be sure I'm dead until you see the crows picking out my eyeballs hanging off the gibbet. Like the man says, it ain't over until it's ov—'

He broke off abruptly as the lumbering Turnbull moved to the top of the stairs as an attractive young woman with shoulder-length brown hair appeared.

'Visitor for you, Quinn,' the man said sourly. 'Again.' He entered the room. Mitch managed to conceal his surprise as the Carrie Clarke he'd met at the Rimfire dance entered the room and crossed directly to the prisoner. Of course he'd heard Quinn had become something of a celebrity and a favourite with the young women of the town, yet Carrie Clarke was obviously a genuine young lady in every sense, and acted like one as she nodded gravely and took his hand formally.

'I heard you were in town to visit with Cody, Mr Reece. I was hoping to hear you might have brought some good news that might help him.'

'Sorry, miss,' he said, glancing at Quinn. 'Matter of fact I guess my visit's been pretty much a waste of time.'

'Nothing's ever wasted, old rancher-bones,' Quinn said, rising from his stool with a clank of chains. 'But who knows? You might get to sit quiet someplace and think over my offer and decide we could do a deal after all.'

'Do you believe Cody is guilty of the things they say he's

done?' the girl asked.

Mitch shrugged.

'I only know what I was asked to do, Miss Clarke. . . .'

He watched her seat herself on a three-legged stool at the outlaw's side. She took something from a pocketbook and he saw it was a bottle of liniment. In a matter-of-fact way she reached out and began dabbing at his many cuts and bruises. It was like she was soothing a savage beast simply by stroking it. Quinn relaxed totally within moments and sat studying her fine-featured face as though in a trance. Watching the couple displaying such warmth and tenderness, Mitch Reece found he had to blink to make certain he wasn't seeing things.

'The marshal says we're to let her visit him in the hope she'll soften him up and mebbe he'll spill to her about the dinero,' the jailer felt obliged to explain to Mitch as they headed downstairs together. 'Talk about pampering! Still, if there's one chance in a million of his lettin' somethin' slip to her. . . .'

'I doubt if the odds are that good.'

'You had no luck, huh? Well, told you you were wastin' your time,' grumped Turnbull, as they reached the lower level to find Marshal Gant standing leaning against an upright, sucking on a cigar. 'Sorry, Marshal.'

Gant slid a bowie from his belt sheath and began paring his nails.

'Too bad,' he grunted. 'Of course I wasn't holding out much hope, but there was still some, I guess.' He didn't look up from his manicure. 'They're not happy with me at Head Office, rancher. They sent me down here to crack Quinn, and I guess I've got to admit I've failed. So, do you know what the marshal's office does with an interrogator that can't interrogate? Uh, huh. They fire him, is what.'

Mitch nodded vaguely. He was studying Gant's hands. The big man's knuckles were scabbed and scarred. Mitch had no sympathy for the prisoner but reacted against this evidence that the man was being systematically brutalizd for any reason.

'I'd better be going,' he said coldly, moving for the exit.

'Did you say goodbye to the prisoner?' Gant asked.

Mitch frowned back at the man as he untied the horse. 'In a way, I guess. Why?'

Gant's eyes were flat and dead-looking. 'Well, you won't be seeing him alive again, that's why.'

'He's going to hang, then?'

'Did I say that? I just said you won't see him again.'

Mitch raised his gaze to the high windows. He suddenly understood what the lawman meant. Gant was prepared to kill the prisoner and there was not a damned thing he could do about it.

With a sour taste in his mouth and a black frown creasing his brows, the rancher headed off to the livery which he reached just in time to come face to face with the livery-man as he came staggering from the building clutching a bloodied forehead.

He couldn't quite believe what the man told him when he recovered his wits. A stranger had entered the livery on some undisclosed business, then apparently caught a glimpse of Lobo in his stall. Claiming to be both a vet and a master judge of good horseflesh, the man had proceeded to check out the mustang while growing steadily more excited, muttering things like, 'I swear he could win the big one carrying the top penalty . . .' and, 'Just look at the depth of that ribcage – born to run forever by God and by Judas!'

He offered to buy the mustang then and there. When

informed it was not his to sell, the stranger turned all silent and pensive. After a time he asked the liveryman to get him a drink of water as he was feeling faint. When the liveryman turned his back something crashed against the back of his head and when he regained consciousness stranger and mustang were both gone.

Coming as it did on the heels of his failure at the courthouse, this latest blow caused Mitch Reece to wonder seriously if he might not be permanently jinxed where his mustang was concerned.

Mrs Gunn heard the clatter of hoofs, the snorting of a hard-ridden horse and a familiar roguish chuckle as she stood at her kitchen bench with arms as red as boiled lobsters buried wrist-deep in sourdough starter.

The wife of the Silver Point vet snorted to herself and gave the sourdough an extra thumping as she heard the opening of the box containing the curry combs and brushes.

If she were to receive just a fraction of all the mollycoddling Gunn lavished so freely upon that half-wild hammerhead stud, she would be in seventh heaven.

That day of course, she well knew, would never come.

That her husband plainly preferred horses to people had been evident throughout their wedded life, yet she had hoped that as they grew older this might change. But instead things went from bad to worse the day that stylish female from Los Robles was passing through and invited Gunn to groom and water her buggy horse while she took her daughter off to lunch.

He fell in love with the horse and had investigated it and its owner and learned to his disappointment the animal was not for sale.

Despite this seeming impasse, he'd insisted he had to have him, and would. Mrs Gunn told him not to be a complete jackass.

Then came the recent day when the horse simply 'appeared' at the Gunn stables and the good woman had to accept the story that it had just shown up, obviously 'neglected and looking for a good home,' as her husband insisted.

Gunn had the mustang out racing his friends next day and was immediately beating everything on four legs over any distance – and Gunn's besottedness was complete.

He'd always craved to possess a truly outstanding horse, and in that unshod and hammerheaded bronco – with teeth that looked like he could chew your leg off – he'd finally found it. Or at least he believed so.

His good lady tried to appear aloof and unaware as he came tramping in with his latest tale of the horse's accomplishments, along with additional information he'd gleaned from a Los Robles horse dealer, passing through.

The man had told him how Grace Bowdre had found Lucky out by Crystal Cliffs with a bullet in him at around the same time that hardcase Kip Petrolle had allegedly killed Sheriff Venture, and had been last sighted hightailing south astride a fleet-footed broomtail.

Gunn found this hint of notoriety only added to the horse's lustre and headed off another wrangle about the animal by wandering outside to feed the hammerhead a biscuit and stroke his aristocratically long nose.

'Goddamned, dad-busted females! What's eating her anyway? I've a good mind to . . .' His voice trailed away and he began stroking the dun's neck. 'What the hell anyway. A woman's just a woman but a horse is a damn good

102

buddy, as they say. You wanna go race the 3.15 coming in, oldtimer?'

'Yeehah!' he yelled, vaulting into the saddle, and with a stutter of hoofs they were gone again. He left his lady brushing the remains of her sourdough from her bench and breaking out the sourmash whiskey.

Poulter lit a cigarette and studied the form guide. Short, fat and smooth in rented suit and patent leather spats, he looked like a wealthy punter enjoying a relaxed day at the races, which was in fact a far cry from the truth. Poulter was doing it tough.

If he didn't win this afternoon he might be obliged to jump the six o'clock southbound to avoid certain creditors.

But it should be simple.

The way he figured, it was just a matter of reading between the lines of the form sheet and using your head.

It all depended on Swift Stepper in the first.

Swift Stepper lost by the length of the straight.

Ten minutes later, Poulter was caught trying to pick a pocket and found himself outside the main gate on his ear with a wild ringing in his head from a regulator's baton.

He closed his eyes and concentrated on the Two Mile Cup.

Poulter sighed and focused on his last hope, the biggest annual horserace from Roswell up to Fort Sumner.

His top lip curled in a bitter sneer as he sat rocking in the westbound train and chewing a dead cigar.

The race was scheduled for the following Saturday and this year he wouldn't even have the fare to get there, let alone hope to come out any kind of winner. He must have dozed. Next thing he knew people were talking and laughing excitedly, and when he opened his eyes everyone was at the windows looking out, pointing and gesticulating.

He turned his pudgy head to see the next winner of the Two Mile Cup slowly overtaking the speeding train on the grassy slopes beyond the right of way. That was how quickly this student of horseflesh assessed the flying dun-coloured broomtail with the paunchy rider bouncing like a ten-gallon jug in the saddle as it drew level with his car and held there for several racing strides before slowly beginning to move ahead.

Poulter was boggle-eyed. Mustangs featured amongst other more fashionable breeds every year at Roswell, and were occasionally amongst the winners. But he knew instantly he had never seen any horse run like this, and just as quickly knew that no matter who owned it, what it was called or where it hailed from, it was going to run in the Cup and he would beg, borrow or steal every last dime to ride on its sturdy back.

When the conductor informed that the hammerhead was from Silver Point, next stop on the line, and belonged to the local vet who liked to race the trains in, it was only a matter of minutes before Merriam Poulter was stepping down on to the tiny platform with a big bogus smile which hid a desperate man ready and willing to go to any desperate lengths to be a winner again, even if it was to be for just one more time.

CHAPTER 7

CLOSE CALL

The Reverend Pearl took a long drink of beer. He wiped his mouth with the back of his hand, shirt-cuffs starkly white against the funereal black of his old-fashioned frock coat. His skin resembled rawhide that had not been soaked properly and the big bulbous nose, all cherry red and shining, made you wonder about his views on absti-nence, considering that he appeared to be so violently opposed to other sins such as murder, banditry and what he classified in Cody Quinn's case as 'all-round bastardry'.

'Very well, my son, I am now restored and ready to hear your confession.' Despite the distraction provided by the travelling preacher man, the prisoner did not seem to hear as he gazed from his window at the big wide day beyond the narrow windows of his Rimfire courtroom prison.

Cody's Window, as all the locals had come to call it, was so named because he had occupied it there for so long now.

He'd come to know a lot about the locals from information grudgingly supplied by the turnkey. He knew who owed money to whom, whose hens weren't laying, which of the three brothers who ran the saloon had been caught beneath the wrong blankets.

On the north side of town stood the blackened ruins of a house that had burned down consuming everyone inside the week before they brought him here, more dead than alive.

Occasionally he sighted his doctor on the street, and whenever he waved the medico waved back. Sometimes when the man was patching him up following more punishment at Gant's hands, Quinn made tasteless jokes about Sheriff Venture having beaten him into the Big Dark, and the older man would grunt but never laughed even though the kid knew he liked him.

Most people did, which was one of the reasons he had survived so long when by all the laws of luck he should have gone to Judgement long ago.

'Might I have your attention, sir?'

The Reverend Pearl was accustomed to receiving full attention. He was six and a half feet tall. Beneath his frock coat he wore chaps, heeled boots, a woollen work shirt and a crucifix on a chain around his neck.

'I have come to shrive your immortal soul before you face your Maker.'

'I never done it.'

'Pardon?'

Cody spread his hands. 'Whatever you've heard, I'm innocent.'

The Reverend was unimpressed.

'Boy, the devil assumes many shapes and manners, his evil to wreak. He'll sneak up on you from behind and take you by the scruff and lead you to hell and gone astray, if he can do it. I believe he has taken you by the hand and led you through pathways and labyrinths most wicked wherein you have left your scarlet trail before the day your sins and villainies finally brought you to this sad place and to the grisly gibbet awaiting you without.'

'Still didn't do it.'

'Damnation, sir—'

'Relax, Uncle,' Quinn said disarmingly. 'Look, we both know why you're here. The marshal can't whip me any worse without killing me, and now his lousy job's on the line on account I won't tell him nothing. So he gets desperate enough to try anything. Like wheeling in an old fraud like you to promise me a ticket to Heaven if I'll just break down and tell you where the money is hid. But I won't. So you're wasting both our time. *Sabe*, Uncle Holybones?'

The preacher rose to full height and clapped the ten-gallon to his bony skull. 'What a sad and sorry waste of a young life.'

'I'll outlive you.'

'I doubt that,' the Reverend said with the solemn air of a man who knew more than he was prepared to say. 'I doubt that very much.' He turned to leave, paused. 'Would you like my blessing?'

'I'm blessed already. Can't you tell?'

Pearl's departing bootheels sounded like the drums of doom. Turnbull crossed the echoing room to look out, talking in low tones to his junior turnkey and occasionally turning to look at the prisoner.

Cody Quinn raised himself on one elbow to look. He sniffed sharply. Suddenly he scented deep trouble.

Gant had been drinking. He could see that the moment the marshal appeared. His big broad face was flushed with liquor and his eyes were mean. His prisoner was no longer a job of work to which he had been assigned. Quinn was now the reason his job and future were on the line.

The Reverend Pearl had been the last shot in the marshal's locker. Menacingly, Gant loomed over the cot. Quinn winked up at him. The lawman went berserk.

Quinn put up a formidable defence as Gant attacked with fist, elbows and knees. He was knocked to the floor but got up again. Gant bashed him into the corner and stood pile-driving punches to head and body until Quinn was bleeding and sliding to the floor. The boot went in but Turnbull found it impossible to haul Gant away.

'Glory, ease up or you'll really kill him, Marshal.'

'What do you think I'm trying to do, you idiot. Leave go of me or you'll be next.'

Matt Gant was out of control and continued to pummel the unconscious prisoner with kicks and blows. Until a voice penetrated his red fog of rage. A big voice. 'Marshal Gant. What the devil do you think you are doing?'

The federal marshal and three deputies from Alameda stood by the bench in travel-stained rig, staring at him.

The reporters from the *Alameda Oracle* newspaper who had accompanied the lawmen to Rimfire were disappointed and angry. Why couldn't they see Quinn, as promised? He was big news and their readers wanted to read what was happening in Rimfire. And why the prolonged delay in his trial?

Was the federal marshal forgetting he had promised they could interview the desperado? They had seen a doctor hurry to the courtroom. Did this mean Quinn was ill? What was going on?

The marshal was calm but firm. There would be no

interview for security reasons. The reporters could wait outside the law office if they wanted. There might be further news they could use later.

The deputies herded the newsmen out and slammed the door. After he was through chewing the turnkey out, the marshal dropped wearily into a chair. He had arrived unannounced to observe for himself why the all-important assignment to force Cody Quinn reveal his cache had failed. He knew the frustrated Gant might well have killed the prisoner had he not been interrupted today. Maybe he could understand this without condoning it. But now things were calmer, the chief marshal was assembling his thoughts and heading towards a major decision.

The prisoner was now a festering sore that must be cauterized.

The region was clamouring for a trial and a hanging, and pressure for this was coming down on Head Office from the Legislature now. The federal marshal's duty was now only too clear.

Due process could not be indefinitely denied for any reason.

Before leaving Rimfire next day he had arranged for the trial of *The People* v. *Cody Quinn* to commence Wednesday of the following week. Nine sharp.

Nobody expected the trial to take long. The authorities had enough evidence against the outlaw to hang him a dozen times over.

Lobo was dreaming.

Standing hipshot in a corner of the horseyard beneath the great stars, the dun was listening to the rolling thunder of the herd beating out its old enthralling rhythm. He could see them now making the night their own, and led by—! Why, it was himself leading them down from the higher lofts of the range as the days shortened. Head held high and yellow tail streaming in the wind, he and the mob were as one, a living river of wild free life streaming over grasslands and dusty stone, running, running because they must and as they would until they were no more.

Then the man.

The mustang grunted in its sleep and the feeling was good as the man who had saved his life and taught him to carry him about on his short back now stroked his muzzle and fed him something good with his fingers.

But now the mob and the man were fading and Lobo moved his head irritably, trying to hang on to the dream despite the little night sounds that were trying to awaken him.

Race day.

'Are you sure you can do this?' whispered Poulter. 'Some of these mustangs will kick a man halfway to hell just to show they feel good.'

'Do you want me to get him or don't you?'

Wrangler was growing testy. The jockey had his suspicions about Poulter and Gunn. They struck him as shifty and over-nervous, and the little man was none too sure about the authenticity of the papers they'd shown him testifying they were the legitimate owners of the animal they wanted him to ride in the Two Mile. Naturally they wanted him to accept the ride on credit. He wanted to tell them to go straight to hell, may well have done so, but for his hunch.

From the moment they'd shown him the mustang named Lucky, Wrangler had had this surprisingly powerful hunch the horse might have what it took.

'You're the best,' Gunn assured him.

'I ain't the cheapest, mister.'

'Five per cent of the prize money,' Poulter said desperately.

'Ten.'

The new partners traded glances. They believed the horse could win. But what they did not believe was that the race stewards would fail, in time, to realize the horse's papers had been forged. So they planned to win, collect the prize money and disappear before paying anybody, including Wrangler.

'A deal,' Poulter promised, and the partners smiled in relief and rushed off to score up every cent they could beg, borrow or steal to plunge on the horse they were entering in the big event under the name 'Bobby Dun' in the next day's Two Mile.

The race was run over a straight open two-mile course and it was the custom of connections of the horses and some of the bigger punters to follow the race in buckboards, buggies and surreys. That Saturday's Cup was no different, with Merriam Poulter in the vanguard of supporters which trailed the racers north.

The race was a test of stamina and speed and the ultimate winner had displayed a wealth of both qualities long before the finish line loomed ahead.

Poulter's hardcase jockey had been nursing his mount throughout this final leg in the belief that the mustang might find something extra when called upon over the final stretch.

So it proved.

The competition fought tooth and nail but were barely able to gallop any longer as the ribbon was broken by

Lobo's sweat-flecked chest.

Poulter was beside himself in the hour that followed, as he was presented with the cup, collected his winnings, posed smilingly for the newsmen with his trophy, with just himself and a huge cigar, with his rider and with winner 'Bobby Dun'.

In the evening there was a big dinner at the Horseman's Room at the Roswell Hotel. The place was crowded and Merriam Poulter was the star guest. It was the biggest night of his life, and with the celebrations continuing into the next day and the one following, he squeezed the moment for all it was worth and had no time at all to sit and deliberate on dull old topics such as the power of the press.

When Mitch came around the front of the house from the tack room, Harry the blacksmith was ringing his anvil with his big hammer across the yard, a haze of smoke drifting towards the horseyards.

He halted.

From here he could see most all of the thirty geldings the hands had been working with over the past week, with fall coming on and the leaves starting to turn. The horses were being fine-tuned to meet the requirements of an army contract he had lined up during the summer.

The geldings looked in prime condition that chilly Tuesday morning, many showing the benefit of Regal Harkeef's bloodline. He spotted the sire watching a couple of 4-year-olds which began trotting along the pasture fence, then milled about nipping at one another, just playing and feeling good.

Reg had an enclosure to himself. He whickered and Mitch whistled back. Since losing Lobo yet again he'd worked with the lofty Arab more and they were closer to being pards than they'd ever been.

But of course there was only one Lobo. Just like there was only one Mary, who now appeared in the doorway and called quite sharply on seeing him 'stargazing' there.

'Mitchell Reece. I'll have you know I've been keeping breakfast warm for twenty minutes.'

Whenever he was 'Mitchell' it was always time to stir his stumps.

He went through to the washroom, scrubbed up, brushed his hair and reached the table just as his wife came through with the steaming breakfast tray. Times like this it was hard to believe they had been married so long. Mary was tall, lithe; a full-breasted beauty by anyone's standard. He could not imagine living here or anyplace else without her. Her thick fair hair cascaded silkily over her shoulders as she took her place, and they were eating and chatting as they did most days when a hand called from out front.

'Buggy just swingin' in, Mitch.'

'Right, Buck.' Mitch rose and went to the window. 'Looks like Morey the storekeeper. What can he want?'

Taking their coffee with them, they walked through to the front as the visitor came through the houseyard gate. The surrey spun dust up behind its brightly painted wheels as the stocky buckskin pony slowed to a trot. Morey, runty, bespectacled and stocky in shirtsleeves, six-button vest and black storekeeper cuffs, popped the reins and urged the little horse along until it was drawing up sharply at the steps.

'Mitch, Mary,' he panted, hopping down clutching a newspaper. 'Sure glad I found you at home, Mitch. This hit my porch less than an hour back and I took it on myself to head straight on out.' He paused on gaining the gallery, holding the newspaper pressed to his chest. 'Ready for a surprise?'

The couple traded smiles. Morey was a great enthusiast for anything that was going, but he seemed unusually excited this morning.

'Solid ready, Morey.'

Mitch meant it. But it turned out he was not quite prepared for the way he felt when the storekeeper turned the paper's front page towards him with a flourish.

There was a headline dealing with a horse race but it was not that which took the eye as immediately as the picture. This depicted a fat man in a tight suit beaming at the camera while clutching a big silver cup with one hand, the other resting proudly on the short breedy neck of a mustang which surveyed the lens with a mixture of aloofness and self assurance.

And Mitch and Mary gasped in unison: 'Lobo!'

CHAPTER 8

FREEDOM IN THE BLOOD

Despite a loafing lifetime spent living on his wits, it often suited Merriam Poulter to view himself as a genuine hard-lucker whom life seemed to single out for rough treat-ment, rather than the failure he really was. Often, but not always.

He was still the toast of Roswell Tuesday morning as, snappy in garish check suit and lime green vest, he swung a valise in his hand and paraded down Lincoln Street heading for the Frontier Livery.

The valise contained some personal effects he had amassed in town, while his billfold was stuffed fat with cash and a stage ticket to Santa Fe. He was anxious now to be on his way before either events or fate might overtake him, as they'd long had a habit of doing.

He had actually stolen another man's horse, and it felt good.

He'd won a big race and a fat pile of cash and it was

time to vanish.

There was one thing he must do first before strolling round to Ash Street and the stage depot; something he didn't have to do, but wanted to.

Lobo was munching oats in his stall. The horse raised its proud head as the fat man sauntered in smelling of lavender water, brandy and whorehouses on this innocent new morning.

Setting down his valise, Poulter dived a hand into his pocket and came up with a fistful of sugar cubes. The horse whickered and came to the stall door to eat them out of his palm with those big teeth that looked as though they could crunch fingerbones like rock candy.

'I'd admire to take you with me, Lucky old boy, but you are better off without me—'

He ceased speaking abruptly.

Lobo's ears were now pricked upright and there was a low sound in his throat while his eyes were fixed at the open doorway. Poulter whirled nervously as a shadow fell across the floorboards and moments later he found himself staring at a tall stranger in expensive range rig and Stetson hat.

And the horse was going crazy.

'Poulter!' the man said in a tone that told the fat man he was in deep trouble. 'What the hell do you think you are doing with my horse?'

Rooted to the spot as Mitch Reece strode into the stables, Poulter felt self-pity roll over him like a tidal wave. Wasn't it always the same? You hit the heights and then came the toboggan ride into disaster and despair.

Yet even as he trembled in his flash patent-leather shoes, the luck, which he always denied ever blessed him, was hard at work. For the horse was now rearing and pawing the air in excitement and Reece strode straight past Merriam Poulter to swing the stall door open, laughing suddenly and calling the broomtail 'Lobo'. He stood hugging its neck as if the fat man did not exist. Wasn't that luck?

And surely it was more luck of the gilt-edged variety that enabled him to tiptoe from the stables and leg it round to Cross Street to be the very last passenger to board the Santa Fe stage before a depot hand slammed the door and the driver cracked his whip over the heads of three span of prancing horses, eager to run.

His real luck of course was the strength of feeling that lay between Mitch Reece and a maverick stud and their reaction to finding one another yet again after each had given the other up as lost.

Neither even noticed the horse-thieving shyster was gone.

'So . . . takin' a good look at your last pretty mornin', eh, kid?' chuckled the turnkey, as he emerged from in back with two pannikins of coffee, just as he had done each morning for many weeks.

No response.

The prisoner stood in Cody's Window gazing out, lost in a dream, the smiling smooth-skinned face as innocent as a choirboy's in the diffused sunlight.

'It's Wednesday, Cody,' he was informed with malicious relish.

Turnbull was disappointed by the continuing lack of reaction he was getting. It would please him no end to have Quinn break down totally now that his life span could be counted in hours, no longer days or weeks. Maybe in a twisted kind of way the turnkey had enjoyed the wild kid's company and the air of excitement that seemed to surround him. And perhaps he'd even gotten to admire the little bastard for the incredible way he'd taken everything Gant could dish out – the arrogant big bastard. But deep down he hated Cody Quinn because, in a hundred subtle ways, he continually reminded Turnbull he was a better man in every way that counted: with horses, with women, with guns and with living every second of his life to the very limit while the turnkey was a 35-year-old going on eighty who had never been anything and never would be.

'Goddamn! Forgot the sorghum!' he said crankily, but the prisoner didn't even turn his head, seemingly mesmerized by the panorama before his window. The fall day was as warm and bright as summer. Late trees and shrubs were in bloom. The kid inhaled the faint fragrance, his ears filled with the drowsy hum of the bees. A chipmunk clucked at him from the branch of the live oak which sheltered the prisoner's 'pets'. He'd watched the pair set up a home in the brush at the base of the tree, had tempted them up higher by placing chunks of bread from his food tray upon the windowsill. Sometimes when Turnbull was drowsing in the judge's chair like a hibernating bear, the prisoner could get the critters to accept food from his hand. He wondered if they would miss him should he get to drop through the trap.

If he should die.

If. . . .

Biggest little word in all creation.

Nobody in Rimfire, Esmeralda County or anywhere in the entire Territory appeared to be in any doubt his execution would take place by sundown today should trial, conviction and sentencing be dispensed as expeditiously as anticipated.

The law had decided it was fed up with Cody Quinn and decided that maybe it was likely well worth throwing away $20,000 just for the satisfaction of seeing the arrogant little bastard walk on this pure autumn air anyway.

But as far as the jail's infamous prisoner was concerned, it was still 'if'.

Cody was yet to hear the fat lady sing.

He was back on his three-legged stool by the cot, with his leg chain angling upwards to the wall hook supporting it at window height, when Turnbull returned with his sorghum. The turnkey was pleased to see the prisoner appeared to have finally snapped out of his reverie as he stirred the two mugs with a tin spoon.

He always made certain to keep well out of Quinn's reach and moved quickly backwards to occupy his own stool. Not once had he taken a single foolish chance with his charge. A man only needed to see Quinn's record in the regional register to sense that just one mistake with this prisoner could well be your last.

'What would you like for breakfast, Cody?' Turnbull asked, tilting his stool back against the wall. With a lazy gesture he fingered the polished stock of his sawed-off, which as always was angled towards the prisoner. 'Mebbe we'd better consider it your last meal, which means you can have anythin' you want.'

'You're really gonna miss me, ain't you, Graff?'

'I see right through you, kid.'

'How's that?'

'Well, you act real easy and casual-like, but you are showin' mighty pale today. In truth, you're lookin' kind of peaked. At last you're gettin' the gyps, waiting for the hangman.'

'I could cure that in about ten seconds.'

'How?'

'Either by cutting Gant's head off or getting a bucking bronco underneath me.'

'You'll buck today, boy, but it will be at the end of a rope. You'll be happy to know the judge and his people arrived late last night. And we expect the chief marshal along later on today. Jimmy Tomms the photographer's been out front of his studio settin' up his paraphernalia and takin' what he calls location shots ever since daybreak. Tells me he wants to get a picture of everythin' and everybody today. Make it into a book and sell it for a dollar a throw. Expects to make a mess of money, so he does.'

'Any more good news for me, Graff?'

The turnkey dropped the front leg of his stool to the floor with a thud, leaned forward confidentially.

'Cody, I got nothin' against you. And I reckon you'd agree I been pretty good to you while you've been here, ain't I?'

'You've been a prince. Except for your mouth of course. And the fact that you just stood by and watched Gant beat the living bejasus out of me about a hundred times. But hell, I don't bear a grudge.'

'I'm glad to hear that,' said Turnbull, the irony going right over his head, 'on account I got somethin' to ask you, boy. Or should I say, ask of you.'

'Wouldn't have anything to do with money, would it, Graff?'

Quinn was smiling but Turnbull could see nothing to laugh about. If cold cash was not a serious subject, what was?

'All that dinero,' he almost drooled. 'Twenty thousand! And everyone knows you stashed it on account you scarce had a dime on you when Venture bagged you so easy at that ranch,' he said in a distant way. 'Let's talk about that cache, kid.'

The boy's face changed alarmingly.

'Let me ask you something, Turnbull. Did you know, slop-gut, that every low-down, motherless, scum-sucking crackerhead who's ever done me wrong, is now dead and gone? I'm not talking some, I'm talking all. Don't that send a chill up your yellow cracker's spine?'

Turnbull was well out of reach. Even so, he still rose and shifted his stool back another couple of feet along the wall, such was the ferocity of that sudden outburst. He was looking at a kid who would not weigh 140 soaking wet, and yet he was afraid – shit-scared all the way down.

'To get back to the money, Cody. I mean, it ain't never goin' to be of any use to you after today, is it? So, well, you know. . . .'

'Why not tell you? Is that what you're trying to say, Graff, old pard?'

'That's right. I'd never forget you if you did.'

'I hope to be remembered. . . .' Cody replied distantly. He rose, yawning and stretching. 'Tell you what, old pard. You go fix me some vittles and when you get back I'll see what I can do for you. A deal? Like you say, you can't take it with you. Eh?'

At last Graff Turnbull found himself grinning like a winner.

This kid, who some claimed to be one part human and nine parts dog-wolf, plainly had a heart after all.

Was it any wonder half the youth of the Territory pinned up pictures of easy-smiling Cody on their walls and wanted to be just like him when they grew up? Turnbull thought benevolently.

'Whatever you say, son,' he beamed, and went off swinging the sawed-off like a baton as he headed down the short hallway behind the juror's bench to vanish in back where pots and pans immediately began to rattle.

Leaving the prisoner sitting motionless on his stool with small hands resting on his knees and the prison-pale face that was still marked darkly by brutal bruising, appearing momentarily, as the turnkey had claimed, 'kind of peaked'. Yet slowly both the prisoner's expression and demeanor changed as he shrugged off a moment's weakening and inward-looking to reallze, in one blinding moment of revelation, that at long last, the hour – his hour – had really finally come, as he'd always known it must.

Suddenly he was upright, dancing on the balls of his feet and eager for action, all the long and intense planning and bouts of uncertainty behind him now. All he had to do was stick to his plan and life would be his for the taking.

And they really believed they could kill him and drop him in an unmarked pit! He knew now he would win. Total certainty could come like that to Cody Quinn at times.

He had practised what he was about to do now countless times whenever left alone up here. He knew he had perfected every angle, every action, every possibility.

It could not fail.

He was as sure of that as he was of life itself and had never felt so sublimely immortal as he did in that fateful moment as he snatched up the chains and went to the wall.

When Turnbull reappeared in the hallway with a fresh mug of sweetened joe to keep his best pal happy while the grub was cooking, he automatically glanced at Cody's corner and dropped the pannikin.

The spectacle that greeted his eye was both grotesque and bizarre.

Somehow in the few minutes he had been out of the courtroom the prisoner must have stood upon his three-legged stool, twisted all the chain slack around his scrawny little neck, looped what was left over the steel barrel hook in the wall, then kicked himself off the stool.

He hung there totally motionless now with his tongue sticking out three inches and unblinking eyes bulging from their sockets, swaying gently like a sack of spuds being unloaded off a palette.

It seemed to a disbelieving Graff Turnbull that the prisoner's face was turning black, the mouth distended in a silent scream, the twisted body and limbs all now perfectly motionless.

'Judas goddamn Priest! No!'

The turnkey rushed forward, cursing and fuming, to jab Quinn viciously in the slats with the shotgun. Quinn swayed violently but showed no sign of life. In a frenzy now the turnkey jumped up on the stool and delivered an enormous kick to the body, still half-hoping it was some kind of trick and he would find the little bastard was faking it.

A faint, strangling wheeze emitted from Quinn's gaping mouth.

The dirty little scut really was still alive!

It seemed to take Turnbull forever to rush across the long room, snatch up a long rod used for closing the curtains at night, charge back and start jabbing at the chain trying to dislodge it from the high wall hook.

He finally succeeded and the limp body crashed to the floorboards with a dead-meat thud.

Motionless.

Turnbull wound up and kicked Quinn viciously in the slats with all his strength. No reaction. And when he stuck his ear near that gaping mouth there was not a whisper of breath.

By this the jailer was sweating furiously, his mind racing like a triphammer. It was true, of course, that they'd planned to kill the bloodthirsty little bastard eventually later on today anyway. But they wanted to do it their way, publicly and fully sanctioned by the law in order to transmit a warning to all the hellions of the Territory, and also because every dignitary in a hundred miles wanted to get to see the outlaw swing.

He whirled towards the hallway, ran a few yards, stopped. He realized that if Quinn wasn't dead already he would be within moments if he didn't get that chain off his neck. And if the bloodthirsty little bastard croaked ahead of time – then who would they blame?

Turnbull, was who.

He rushed back, grabbing furiously at the chain and attempting to make the prisoner sit up so he might work on his chest. But the slack, seemingly boneless body proved so infuriatingly difficult to manage, that by the time a vital half-minute had passed, Graff Turnbull realized there was only one thing left to do.

He had to loosen that freaking chain somehow before he did another damn thing! Ten lunging strides took him to the keyring hanging on the plastered wall at the hallway entrance. Snatching it down, he sped back to the corner beneath Cody's Window. He groaned when he saw that the contorted face appeared to be in exactly the same frozen death-mask contortion as before, tongue protruding, eyes staring sightlessly. He could count every tooth in the gaping jaws. 'Don't be dead, you spotty-faced piece of

124

shit!' he raged, fumbling with key and padlock. 'Gant will have my balls. I shoulda known you were all talk . . . couldn't face your fate like a man . . . ahh . . . got it!'

The padlock snapped open and dropped to the floor but the body lay limp and lifeless as ever. Kneeling now, Turnbull feverishly tore at the chain loops wrapped around the neck, and they now seemed much looser than before. Working with manic haste, sweating and cursing like a muleskinner, he suddenly experienced a chilling sensation as though someone or something was staring at him.

He jerked his head to look across the room.

No.

Nobody there.

His gaze cut back to the 'dead man' and he froze. Quinn's eyes were wide open! The killer was staring straight up at him with mirth twinkling in those sky-blue eyes now, mouth beginning to curl upwards in that all too familiar grin.

Turnbull's heart tried to fly out of his mouth.

Then every muscle in the big body exploded into motion and he was twisting from the hips in the kneeling position, his big left hand pawing at the prisoner to try and hold him down while his free hand grabbed for the sawed-off propped against the wall so tantalizingly close.

His left hand was parried aside and next instant an incredulous Turnbull felt the leg chain whip around his neck like a bull snake, biting into the flesh, cutting deep.

But he was a big man and strong.

Hands flying to the chain, he threw his body backwards seeking to dislodge his attacker. He failed. Quinn allowed himself to fall on his back to the floor with the turnkey atop him. For one leaping moment as Turnbull sought to clamp all his power and weight down upon the chain still stretched across the neck of the outlaw beneath his great bulk, he actually believed he'd won. That Cody Quinn's last-minute roll of the life dice had come up snake eyes. Then the moment was gone and Turnbull's eyes were trying to jump out of their sockets as, with a length of the chain twisted around both his hands, Quinn exerted full lethal pressure which cut off the windpipe and had the big body flopping about like a dying fish, pounding at him furiously but not hurting any.

Nothing could hurt him now. Nobody.

The universe was slowly darkening in Turnbull's vision. He realized dimly his back was now against the floor and that the killer was above him, one knee jammed into his chest, chain-knotted hands red with the blood spilling from the turnkey's tortured throat spewing out of his mouth.

The outlaw leaned close, his face like a shining wet knife-blade.

'*Adios amigo.* Too bad you gotta go, Graff, on account this here turkey shoot is just fixing to open.'

And he jerked on the crossed chain with such savagery that blood spurted from his jailer's gaping jaws to soak his shirt front and Turnbull's brain went dead in one blinding white flash of oblivion.

It was some time later as, hitching at his gun-belt and chewing on a toothpick, Marshal Matt Gant quit the Greasy Skillet eatery to make his way across Rimfire's long main street for the courthouse.

The marshal had eaten well for he was anticipating a long and challenging day ahead, although naturally it would be preferable to be able simply to stand in this nice warm autumn sun and watch that mad-dog killer hang high, wide and handsome.

The hangman from Alameda had arrived yesterday and had been quite proud and willing to afford the marshal his first up-close look at a hangman's rope and knot. Not the regular slip-knot cattlemen employed when lynching rustlers and suchlike; a real professional piece of work, and of course the knot was all-important as the hangman had been at pains to explain.

'Good stout manilla, of course, Marshal. The only hangrope worth a damn. And see my knot? Got seven turns to it. The rope slips through it smooth as quicksilver. Right up under the jawbone this baby goes, crunches the Adam's apple like a nut and snaps the spine like a dead twig. Never had me a failure yet.' Gant was comforted by the knowledge that prosecutor, judge, jury and executioner would all do what was expected of them. But while one part of him exulted at the pure finality of what was to befall his youthful tormentor, he realized that after it was all over, he still must come face to face with the reality of his own waning star.

His title of special marshal was a pseudonym for official torturer. When they had bestowed it upon him they'd given him the full unspoken responsibility of forcing Quinn to talk, and his failure in that direction must forever cast a shadow over his future.

Yet the closer he drew to the courthouse-cum-prison the more easily he was able to focus on the here and now and less on incidentals. 'Today's only reality will be Quinn's curtain call, Marshal,' he reminded himself emphatically. 'Squeeze full pleasure out of that and worry about anything else later.'

He planned to go directly to the courtroom and take

the stairs to the second-storey porch. His eyes kept sweeping the building as he approached. All was quiet.

The open windows of the upper floor were empty, no sign of a fair head in Cody's Window today. He would like to picture finding the outlaw with his head hidden under his pillow, blubbering like a baby, yet didn't really fancy his prospects. If the hardcase breed ever came any tougher than Quinn he'd never encountered it.

He was slow to realize the road was deep in dust. This would mess up the fine shine on his boots he'd worked up. The day was so clear and sunny it was almost hot for this late in the year. The crab apple tree at the corner of the courthouse seemed to droop a little under the sun. He passed through its dappled shade and took just one step beyond into the sunlight again.

'Morning, Marshal.'

The killer's voice!

Friendly and casual.

Very close.

Gant's blood seemed to turn into ice crystals and he was jerking revolver from holster as his head snapped back violently to stare straight upwards into the yawning black barrels of a sawed-off shotgun now angling down from Cody's Window. Above the glinting metal surfaces of the shotgun was Cody Quinn's narrow face dominated by unblinking blue eyes that appeared to smile down upon him as though with genuine affection.

All the time the marshal was raising his service revolver.

But something was wrong.

The weapon weighed a ton and his arm felt like it was locked in a vice. His heart beat wildly in a way he'd never experienced before. It felt as if there was a desperate bird named terror inside him attempting to burst its way out of his big barrel-chest as he tried to cry out, to curse, to damn God – to demand he be allowed let live!

But no sound escaped his mouth and he was still fighting to get his frozen limbs to do his bidding, his eyes still locked with the kid's, when Quinn jerked both triggers.

All Rimfire heard the shuddering double discharge of lead and gunpowder which all but blasted Gant's head from his shoulders. A gush of acrid blue gunsmoke drifted lazily off into the street.

Eighteen pieces of buckshot had struck the marshal at point-blank range, yet some convulsive final stiffening of limb and sinew held his body upright for what seemed an unconscionably long time in which men began pouring from the buildings, only to freeze at the sight that greeted their eyes.

A strangely familiar headless figure sprawled in the deep dust of the street with a ghost fog of gunsmoke drifting away.

That was shocking enough.

But far worse was the sight of Cody Quinn descending the outside staircase with a big country-boy smile stitched across his face, both hands empty now but with two big revolvers thrusting upwards from the broad shell-belt buckled around slim hips as he jumped to the ground. He continued to saunter casually around the building corner before finally breaking into a jog that carried him along the lane leading towards the blacksmith's.

Cody was chuckling.

All his preparation had paid off in aces! He'd had his heady successes in the past, yet nothing could compare with this and he laughed out loud suddenly thinking of how brilliantly he'd plotted and executed big-bellied Turnbull – exactly as he'd planned in every detail.

By contrast, the decision to kill Gant had been prompted by opportunity but had paid off in a way that left him breathless with pure joy.

He knew that when he eventually made it to South America with his twenty thousand he would spend many a long sunny siesta dreaming of how both swaggering badge-packers had succumbed to him so meekly in the end. Like it had always been destined to play that way – and he knew he would never grow weary of reliving their final moments in the theatre of his mind even should he survive to become the oldest Yankee expatriate in Rio.

Ducking swiftly along to the smith's, as curious citizens flocked into the main street to puzzle about the gunshots, he found three horses, one saddled. The blacksmith all but passed out when he finally emerged from his forge alcove to investigate the sound of shots, only to come face to face with a man he'd only ever seen over the long weeks gazing down from the high window above the courthouse.

From Cody's Window!

'Take it easy and you'll live to see your grandkids, Pops.'

The smith froze as though his boots had sprouted deep roots. He did not even turn as the outlaw casually forked the saddled horse, scooped up the tether ropes of the other two animals and galloped off down a side steet and away from the slowly awakening town.

The chief marshal and his escort gave immediate chase but were never in danger of catching him. He took remounts with him and they didn't.

CHAPTER 9

HUNT THE
MAN DOWN!

Lights blazed from every window of the ranch house in the three o'clock chill of early morning. Behind the misted windows which threw diffused lamplight over the steaming horses lined up at the Mustang Ranch hitch rail, a council of war was in progress.

The council comprised some fifteen prominent Rimfire citizens including sheriff and mayor, and the battle they were involved in was the same one which had been fought and lost before on two occasions: once when Cody Quinn fled through here and up into Shattuck Range with his bank haul, and again when he'd finally quitted the high lonesome to steal the mustang stallion back and make his almost fatal visit to Rooney Ranch.

Every man in that smoke-filled room believed Quinn must now be headed this way again, and that included Mitch Reece. The fact that the fugitive had not been sighted since giving his Rimfire pursuers the slip strengthened the conviction that the desperado had to be heading back up to Shattuck Range to collect the cached bank loot as a prelude to finally quitting the Territory, which posed the big question.

How did you counter a man so tricky and lethal that even the full force of the law seemed incapable of nailing him? Everybody knew the Shattucks grew progressively more forbidding the higher you climbed. The delegation here was looking to Mitch's expertise and local knowledge of the wilderness to assist them snare the outlaw. Yet again. He had been hunting the wild horses of Shattuck Range for ten years and more and knew them intimately and it seemed to him that his visitors expected him to figure out which route he believed Quinn would be most likely to take upon once clearing the rangelands and heading for the Shattucks and possibly Silverado Plateau – the high range of the mustangs.

'That wouldn't be all that easy to figure even if we knew where the money is cached – that's if it's still up there,' Mitch answered quietly. 'But as we don't it's plain as a pikestaff. He could take any trail of a dozen.' This triggered off a storm of debate.

Mitch eventually slipped from the spacious front parlour and made his way through to the music room where Mary sat at the piano, not playing, just sitting there with her hair lying loose on her shoulders, eyes tense and worried. 'I don't want you to go, Mitch,' she stated flatly. 'They have no right coming here to you, again. You went up to Rimfire for them because they didn't have anyone with the gumption even to talk to this killer. Now, as soon as he breaks out, they are up here looking to you to risk your life and try and get their silly money back for them. I won't allow you to do it. I really won't.'

He sat down in a deep chair of black leather with a cigar

in one hand and a coffee mug in the other, the picture of a man of the land taking his ease. But of course he was far from that. He knew what he must do, but the tough thing to do first was convince his wife.

'Honey,' he said, 'he'll come. He was making this way when he quit Rimfire. He's afraid of nothing. And the simple fact that none of the bank money has turned up since he quit the range means it's got to be still up there.'

'But, Mitch, you—'

'He'll come, men will try to stop him, and good men will die, Mary. It's that simple. The fact that I know the range just about better than anyone, and that I've met Quinn and so at least have a pretty clear idea of what we're up against, means that I'm most qualified to hunt him. And if I stood back and looked on while more good men got hurt or killed, knowing I could have helped. . . .' He shook his head. 'I don't think I could live with that, honey. I doubt you could either if it comes to that.'

It was a hard moment for Mary Reece for she was a woman of the land who understood the danger involved in what her husband was proposing. He had spent much of his life hunting horses; now they wanted him to go hunting a man. And not just any man, but a ruthless killer who had demonstrated time and time again his ability to survive at any cost, a talent most recently evidenced at Rimfire Jail.

She shuddered.

All she had ever wanted was a simple life here in the country with the horses and the man she loved. She might have attempted to dissuade him from joining the posse had she known him less well. But Mitch Reece was not the kind to turn his back on people who needed him. And this was further reinforced by the fact that, like the mayor and

133

sheriff, she knew that should Cody Quinn return to the Range as everyone expected, then the very best man to pursue him or try to snare him was that man who knew the region best, her husband.

'All right, darling,' she said finally with a calm she was far from feeling. 'Do what you feel you must. But promise me one thing, that you won't take any reckless chances.'

He kissed her, then kissed her again.

Unlike some amongst the posse who were acting eager and excited at the prospect of coming to grips with the outlaw, Mitch was deeply apprehensive at what lay ahead.

Once before Quinn had defied the concentrated efforts of scores of manhunters to dig him out of the higher levels of the range for a lengthy period of time when half the county was combing the brush hunting for him. He was a killer who would not hesitate to take life again should he feel threatened. And last and most significantly, Mitch had met him and felt the power of his personality and sensed what he was capable of.

Quinn might well be little more than a youth but he was the most dangerous man Mitch Reece had ever encountered.

A man could get himself killed.

Thrusting that thought aside, he hugged his wife urgently and returned to the parlour.

The possemen were hugely relieved to hear his decision, and took comfort from his air of calm confidence as he spread the sheriff's map out on the dining table and began to outline the situation as he saw it. If he was apprehensive about what lay ahead he was determined not to let it show at this time.

'I've always had a notion about Quinn's last visit here the time he stole my stud and just disappeared,' he said.

'And that was that he made his way up to Cloud Plateau and Paiute Cliffs and found himself a hideaway up there someplace, although God alone knows where. I've combed the region maybe a dozen times without coming up with a damn thing. But on account that's the part of the Range where I'd look to hide out if I had to, then I still reckon we should concentrate our work there. Or to start with, at least.'

The others studied the map which clearly showed the two-to-three mile plateau curving from north to south below the jagged line of the Paiute Cliffs, as well as the two canyons by which access to the plateau was possible, the Fork Creek and Dano's Canyon.

Mitch traced the canyons with his finger.

'I've been thinking on what I said about which route Quinn might take, and maybe I've narrowed it down some now. If my hunch has any weight, and Quinn is making for the plateau in a big hurry, then I reckon he'll likely try one of the canyons to reach Paiute Cliffs rather than ride a hell of a long distance north where the plateau peters out into low sloping country and is accessible from there.'

He paused to look at each face in turn.

'We're a dozen strong. So my suggestion is we split in half and post ourselves at the mouth of each canyon, lie low and just see if we mightn't snare our man coming in. What do we think?'

It took some time to decide on this, for to some the plan seemed a passive patient way of going about their task when some of the more impulsive saw themselves flushing the fugitive, giving headlong pursuit and doubtless taking him dead or alive in a blaze of gunsmoke glory.

But the sober heads eventually prevailed, and it was agreed the sheriff should command one bunch to cover

Fork Creek while Mitch would be entrusted to command the Dano's Canyon party.

With agreement reached, there was no reason for delay in getting mounted and heading out. Latest information and guesswork placed Quinn at a still considerable distance westward from the spread. But Mitch nonetheless insisted they make the ride up to the canyons at the gallop in the event their quarry should throw all caution to the winds and make one desperate, headlong rush to make it to the Range under cover of darkness ahead of the posse.

It would seem a prudent precaution to take in light of what was known of the killer's patterns. Yet at the very moment the posse quit the Mustang Ranch's home acres, with Mitch Reece leading them astride his dun stud, Cody Quinn was lounging back in total comfort in a warmly lamplit adobe twenty miles from Rimfire, washing a huge plate of chili con carne down with a mug of scalding coffee and idly stroking the soft brown hair of the lovely young girl beside him while a swarthy range-rider with a thick Mexican accent was advising him how he best might get to make his way around the lines of the possemen in order to reach the high country safely.

'*Vaya con Dios*, Cody!' called the *vaquero*, who worked for the only rancher in the region who hired Mexicans exclusively. His voice was soft and musical in the night. 'Go with God, and may God protect you from our enemies, *por favor.*'

'Our' enemies, the man had said.

Not just the enemies of killer Cody Quinn but all those many enemies of the poor and uneducated have-nots, such as these ranch workers. For only the lawless, the losers or the truly lost looked up to men like Quinn, who seemed to have the courage and ability to challenge the rich and powerful whom the poor envisioned as ranked against them, as likely they were.

Such people identified with Cody while he simply made use of them on occasion. Such was the case tonight when he'd come seeking sanctuary after recklessly visiting the Clarkes every evening then taking 'his' girl this far with him.

'*Hasta*, old man,' the slim rider called back. Then looked down at the girl he loved clutching his stirrup leather and gazing up at him and fighting back the tears. The Mexicans wanted to believe the *caballero*-outlaw might return one day and carry the ranchero's daughter away to a romantic new life where nobody would want to kill him, unlike here where everybody seemed eager to do so if given half a chance. But until then it was, '*Adios*, Billy. Take care, *hombrecito*.'

And from Carrie, 'Go with God, my darling boy.'

He just grinned cockily.

He'd never relied on God or anyone else . . . before her, that was.

Cody always took care of Cody when the chips were down. And he was doubly confident he would make it now, with his belly filled with the fine Mexican-cooked vittles and his head filled with plans on how best he might make it back up into Shattuck Range despite just about every towner, bounty-hunter and lawman in the region being out hunting for him this wild and windy night.

Just the one horse now with the mounts he'd worn out running from Rimfire left behind with his grateful host. This gelding was full of running and it carried him away swiftly along the backtracks and animal pads the Mexican had identified for him, halting occasionally when distant riders were sighted, hurrying on only when they had safely passed.

Hurrying for Dano's Canyon as it was the ideal route up to Paiute Cliffs at Cloud Plateau, the hideaway and the money.

He threw his head back and laughed aloud. How patient, how cunning and just plain lucky he had been all this long time.

His enemies could neither understand him nor deal with him. He kept proving he had the edge and would do so again when he recovered the money, crossed into Mexico and set up the dynasty Cody Quinn.

With her, of course.

Carrie Clarke, daughter of well-to-do Roger and Hyacinth Clarke and soon-to-be the wife he would love truly until the day he died – from old age, of course. His survival and escape might well in time prove to be the stuff of legend and folklore, but for him the girl and what she had done to him and for him was the impossible story. He'd never loved anybody until he'd visited the stage station at Morgan's Flat that day and a pretty and highly intelligent young woman had grabbed him by the heart.

He thought he'd half forgotten her until she'd visited him in Rimfire Jail. That visit, and all those that followed, had given him the resolution to survive and triumph, he knew.

They were like innocent young lovers together – him, innocent! Yet that was how he felt when they were together. And he believed he must be destined to survive, get the cache, set up a new life and send for her – just like folks did in those romantic novels he never got to read.

He could have it all if he could just stay alive.

At the end of his climb he stood by his horse in a stand of peppercorns at the mouth of Dano's Canyon, and burned with silent rage as he disbelievingly watched the dim figures riding along the the high-walled creek below.

Possemen!

Some sharp-head had figured he would try to take the shortest way up to Shattuck's Range, and so they'd strung a line across Dano's. Doubtless it would be the same along at Fork Creek Canyon, which meant simply he would have to settle for Dano's and take his chances here.

The two-hour wait until the possemen had bedded down for the night and the canyon grew quiet were long, but nowhere near as long as the murderous stretches he'd put in at Rimfire Jail, he told himself.

It was the best part of an hour before he was ready.

When he finally quit the trees, the outlaw was afoot and had ditched boots, sawed-off and anything metallic which might scrape and give him away.

This was challenge territory for Cody Quinn, but his ego kept reminding him that he couldn't think of one other man capable of pulling it off.

Of course he could simply quit and lie low, he realized. Hole up someplace for a couple of weeks, then try again after these crummy manhunters had quit and gone back down to the rangeland.

The hell with that!

He'd done the impossible in both surviving Rimfire and busting free. He could make it three in a row standing on his hat!

He now proceeded to prove his own brag, threading his bare-footed way between blanket-shrouded sleepers and skilfully eluding two sentries east of the camp.

He was clear of all but the remuda now. It was guarded,

but nothing would have prevented him snaking into the draw where the horses dozed in a circle with two half-asleep townsmen with rifles seated slumped on a hollow log.

A minute later the nighthawks lay unconscious side by side on the damp grass and the outlaw was holstering his Colt before working his lithe-hipped way in amongst the horses. He'd glimpsed the tall figure of Mitch Reece from a look-out point earlier and was excited by the prospect of snatching the stallion yet again and in so doing deliver a blow to his reputation.

He should have been climbing but instead stood indecisively, staring off at the barely visible remuda, where he'd glimpsed the unmistakable shape and hue of the mustang stallion less than an hour before.

He knew what he was thinking was crazy. But he'd been doing the crazy and the impossible all his life. He fingered his gunbutts and grinned like a wolf. He could simply recover his cache and vanish along his secret trails here, making these lawdogs look bad – or he could steal the mighty mustang from under their noses and make Reece look a fool forever.

A flitting ghost in the night, he snaked off in the direction of the remuda making no more noise than a passing zephyr.

Lobo was not there!

Upon making this discovery, the killer's fury almost overwhelmed him and he was nearly loco enough to consider going back down and finding wherever that crafty Reece had stashed his precious hack – before the unexpected saved him from committing a possibly fatal error of judgement.

He heard steps and a voice. Whirling away from the

140

weary horses he suddenly came face to face with the startled posseman who'd come up from the main camp below, rounding a patch of thornbush.

The man was startled and Quinn rattlesnake quick as he whipped the knife from his belt and buried it haft-deep into the Rimfire blacksmith's heart. Then he vaulted across the nearest horse's sturdy back and set off for the Paiute Cliffs and a hidden speck in the higher Shattucks called the Crater. He asked himself buoyantly, what did he need with any fool bronco when he had $20,000 almost within reach?

'What are you doing, man?' the sheriff asked querulously. It had been a terrible night, what with blacksmith Gus Walsh being found dead, all stiff and stark under the moon with a knife sticking from his chest, and later the discovery of an abandoned horse, weapons, a set of boots and other clues identifying their owner as Cody Quinn who'd encroached to within a stone's throw of their heavily guarded campsite.

The sheriff felt he had failed here at Dano's Canyon and was anything but cheered by the spectacle of Mitch Reece calmly studying one of the small, high-heeled bootprints in the soft earth. Then his mustang suddenly began sniffing at the ground and rolled its eyes eloquently at its master. Plainly the animal had picked up the scent and a ripple of emotion ran through the men, some suddenly white with apprehension but an equal number reacting positively, eager to get riding.

'He's got his scent,' Mitch affirmed quietly. 'Lobo knows Quinn's scent, and he also knows the Shattucks. We'll let Lobo lead us to him.'

The sheriff stared at the mayor, who looked blankly

back at him and grunted, 'Huh? Are we fixing to follow a horse now?'

'They can follow a scent better than a watchdog, this breed,' grunted Mitch. 'Quinn had him for quite a spell, so he recognizes his scent, that's for sure. Could save us a lot of time and miles in the long run.'

This was meant to encourage, yet seemed to have the opposite effect upon some. This posse had left the rangeland strong, committed and united in purpose. But the best part of a day's brutal and at times risky climbing ever higher in Reece's wake had taken the edge off even the most resolute, while the very strangeness and isolation of this eerie high country had done nothing to boost flagging spirits.

But what had happened here sometime during the night had chilled all but the toughest when they realized the man they were hunting had walked right through them as they slept!

Any one of them might have awakened by chance and looked up into the boyish smiling features of Cody Quinn might even have gotten to hear him whisper, 'Sleep tight, Judas!' before his bowie knife slit his throat ear to ear.

One man had already been savagely murdered and now the man they hunted had made his way up through them to reach familiar Shattuck Range where he had previously successfully survived all attempts to flush him out. Urgency was in the air but doubt was rampant. And confident in Mitch Reece though they were, many were beginning to suspect that his iron determination to press on up into the dangerous country now was proof of his affection for his ugly bronco rather than anything more relevant.

The mayor began to complain but Mitch's voice cut him off mid-sentence. 'Shut up. All of you shut up.'

This startled them for Mitch was regarded as the calmest of men even when under pressure.

But they didn't understand the pressure he was feeling now – had been feeling ever since the discovery of the blacksmith's corpse and footprints in damp grass.

They had all been eager to follow him then but now Gus Walsh had followed him to his doom.

Mitch understood their mood but nothing would stop him now. He no longer simply wanted to snare Quinn; now he knew he must.

And the posse would ride with him.

He told them so in a handful of words, and not a single man dared challenge him now they read the look in his eyes as he swung astride his mustang to lead them eastwards along the canyon creek then upwards for the plateau.

There were no tracks up here; the outlaw had left none. Their only hope now lay either in Lobo's keen nose or blind luck, otherwise Cody Quinn must come out a winner yet again.

CHAPTER 10

THE WILD ONES

Mitch Reece now rode alone.

His exhausted companions had finally rebelled against their trailsman and signreader after he'd insisted on back-tracking the plateau for the third time. In doing so he was plainly demonstrating more confidence in the tracking skills of his hammerhead than in the logic of maintaining a wide and intense search pattern elsewhere other than an area they'd already thoroughly covered to no avail ... twice.

This time Mitch rode even more slowly than before, halting frequently to scout around afoot, to look and listen, noting Lobo's reaction to various specific sites and pathways as had not been possible when travelling with the bunch.

He was also working on the belief that the horse's sense of smell – having been exposed to the killer's footprints – might be best exploited to the full without the distracting odours of so many men and animals to confuse the scent. The day was clear and the high country was quiet now.

From time to time through gaps in the trees, cliffs and fissures away to his right, he occasionally caught glimpses of the tiny dots of other searchers far below combing the distant plains.

To his left, the gnarled and heroic loft of Paiute Cliffs threw shadows across the tortured landscape. He rode on with his gaze cutting restlessly from side to side, searching for tracks he wasn't sure he might ever find. His quarry had made it up here both alone and barefoot, suggesting he might now be leaving behind no more sign than a leaf blowing across solid stone. Mitch studied the rearing cliffs looming above. He believed he recalled most of them from his previous manhunt for Quinn earlier in the year. He was suspiciously studying a huge rearing clump of thorny brush directly ahead when Lobo suddenly pricked his ears, eyes cutting left and upwards. For just a moment Mitch felt a jolt of optimism as he hauled the stud to a halt. Then he felt a chill run through him as he saw the reason for the horse's distraction.

Standing on a lofty rim some two hundred feet above them, and looking as wild and handsome as though they were consciously posing against the hot New Mexico sky, a pair of wild horses, a colt and a white-socked filly stood gazing imperiously out over their kingdom.

As man and horse stared upwards, the filly tossed her pretty head and nipped the colt's arched neck playfully. He jumped, tossed his head, and then both swept away, gliding effortlessly over the rugged earth beyond the rim, seeming almost to fly as lightly as creatures made of light and air rather than flesh and blood.

A deep shudder ran through Lobo's entire frame and for a moment the man felt attuned to his horse in a more intense way than he'd ever experienced before. Lobo had been the strongest and truest horse he'd ever ridden, a boon companion reliable as the sunrise. Yet he still had the heart of a wild broomtail, something which could never change, and the man understood the reason why what they had just seen might still powerfully arouse the stallion even after years of domesticity.

The moment quickly passed.

There was a job to be done and man and horse continued doing it for another hour which took them a thousand feet higher, south past both the canyons then on to yet another familiar stretch of plateau, high and broken yet studded with good solid trees and a scattered array of giant boulders that had fallen down off the cliffs over the ages.

He was walking and leading the horse when Lobo suddenly tossed his head and began half-turning, facing the cliff face. Mitch looked to see that the stud's attention was focused on a stand of live oaks growing closely together, hard against a granite wall as though for protection.

'Nothing up there,' Mitch said quietly. 'I've searched that quarter before.' But the horse continued to jerk on its bit and flare its nostrils. Eventually Reece gave in and they set off up the sharp climb.

Up close, the trees appeared exactly as Mitch remembered, and he would have pushed on impatiently had not Lobo again began acting strangely as he had done lower down, this time flaring his nostrils and sniffing loudly in a way that sent a sudden jolt of excitement rippling along Mitch's spinal column. Surely the animal was trying to tell him something?

Quickly he swung down, and the mustang actually nodded its head and rolled its eyes at him as though in approval of his decision.

Before moving a step he drew his sixgun and double-checked the loads before replacing it in the holster. He looked up into the horse's eyes which were now stretched to their maximum.

'Cody?' he whispered.

But this was asking too much of any animal, even this one. Lobo just shook his head then rolled his eyes back towards the tree clump – but that was more than enough for his master.

'Stay put!' he ordered as the stallion made to follow him. 'This isn't any dumb horse-trapper we're looking for, oldtimer. I'll take it from here.'

The animal appeared to understand, even if it halted with obvious reluctance as he walked away.

The cliff wall loomed massively overhead as he finally turned to move along its base. Here the ground was thickly overgrown and he could understand why he'd not investigated farther here before, where heavily leafed branches had been forced either downwards or upwards after coming into contact with the rock to form a seemingly impassable tangle of vegetation. From even up close it still appeared there wasn't so much as a crack or fissure in the overgrown rock face.

He shot a questioning look back over his shoulder. Lobo stood a hundred feet below, watching him intently. The horse seemed to nod its big hammerhead. Encouraged, Mitch moved onwards along the cliff base for a short distance before hearing the animal whicker.

He halted with a frown as he approached a dense-growing section, then thought he glimpsed something beyond. He pressed closer to a huge gnarled tree-trunk, reached up and dragged a pliant branch aside.

His heart skipped one full beat then began to trot.

Before him now lay a fissure wide enough to ride a horse through, slicing away at a sharp angle to curve behind a knife-edged façade of grey stone which made it impossible to see beyond. He pressed quickly on until glimpsing shafts of sunlight streaming down into what appeared to be a tight little basin beyond. He whirled to stare down at the horse and Lobo's eye met his with a lively look, and the man licked dry lips.

Of course this could still prove to be nothing, he knew. But just as easily it could mean he'd stumbled on to a well-concealed hideaway.

Checking out his Colt for the final time, Mitch realized the game had changed. His tingling spine proclaimed it and the dryness in his mouth affirmed it. It was like all the outdoor instincts he'd developed and honed over the years were trying to tell him of something significant here.

There was only one way to be sure.

He felt a chill as he took his first step into the mouth of the fissure.

He knew the prudent thing to do was to go mount up and go racing off to locate the possemen to back his play. Sensible. But how much time might he have, demanded his mind. Just say that Cody was in there right now. Were he to return to get the posse, the outlaw could quit the hide and be long gone – maybe even with the Rock Creek Bank haul – before he could return.

That was a risk he dare not take. Couldn't risk losing the money – if it still existed anyplace. Nor could he risk allowing Cody Quinn to give him the slip and maybe get to kill, kill and kill again.

Which left no alternative.

He saw an imaginary billboard in his mind's eye

announcing the programme: Mitch Reece versus Cody Quinn!

What would be the gamblers' odds posted back in Rimfire if that were the announced bill of entertainment? How could the outlaw be at anything but long odds-on to come out the winner?

It was eerily quiet padding forward between rearing walls of stone, cool and gloomy. Then he went down on one knee to peer through a screen of brush into the tight little basin nestled here unseen and unsuspected with just a small patch of blue sky visible high above; the sound of gurgling water lending the place a cloistered and placid atmosphere.

He sniffed woodsmoke.

Dropping flat, he belly-wriggled forward until he could make out the sturdy lean-to on the far side of a gently burbling rock spring. Smoke curled from a tiny fire at which the hunched figure of a man in yellow shirt and big hat sat with his back towards him.

Mitch licked his lips and cocked his .45.

Trying to remember all the stealthy tricks he'd picked up over years spent hunting the mustangs, he sucked in a deep intake of breath, thought of Mary then rose in a crouch and began to move forward.

'Well, if it ain't the rancher again.'

His head jerked up violently almost jinking his neck.

The smiling face of Cody Quinn stared down at him from a leafy ledge directly above the entrance to the hideaway. There was a sixgun in the outlaw's right hand, and even though Mitch saw the finger tighten on the trigger and the murderous glitter of the eye, he continued to jerk his own piece upwards, determined to shoot it out, sure he was about to die but determined at least to die fighting.

A flicker of alarm spread across the killer's face which Mitch didn't understand immediately. For instead of cutting loose and shooting him down where he stood, Quinn instead launched himself off his ledge with incredible speed, bare white feet slamming into Mitch's head and shoulders before he could pull trigger.

They crashed to the ground and Mitch was a fraction slow bringing up his weapoon. Quinn's gun slammed against the side of his skull and he felt himself rolling, his head filled with shooting stars.

By the time he sat up, Quinn had his Colt thrust into his belt and was standing over him with feet wide-planted, his own revolver cocked and angled at his face. He couldn't help but notice that the man was not even breathing hard. Characteristically, he was smiling down on him again with those even white teeth.

'You really are something, Mitch. I figured all I had to do was wait here until dark, then hightail. Reckoned if I couldn't make the border by daybreak I must be in the wrong business. But tell me, horseman, how'd you squirrel me out? Hell! I was up here two months afore and nobody came even close to finding me here. You can't say I left any tracks, as I know I never.'

Mitch got to his feet.

The other made no attempt to stop him.

Mitch gazed around, focusing on the clever effigy the killer had set up across the spring by the lean-to, which had so comprehensively deceived him. Quinn laughed softly.

'I had that old dummy still set up across there from the last time, rancher. Some set-up, huh? Never knew for sure if I was safe here, so I set that figure up to fool any sonuva who might stumble in, while I spent most of my time keeping watch on my ledge up above with a good blanket and my guns, recovering from the slug I took on my runout from Rimfore after I hit the Rock Creek Bank. And I can just see what you are thinking, so I'll set your mind at rest. Yeah, the dough's been here all the time. Before I ducked back down to Esmeralda County to visit with Rooney at his ranch, I was plenty lonesome, make no mistake. But I also wanted to test the waters down below in the county – you know, figure if I could make it to Mexico with the dinero or not. Found out I could've, only old Venture had other notions. Want to see the haul before we hightail?'

'We?'

'Sure. Like I said, I was ready to wait until dark. But now I've got me such a big-note hostage, I reckon it's as good as a free ticket to the border. I expected you to have figured that out for yourself after I jumped on you instead of blowing your head off.' The smile vanished to reveal the man behind the boyish mask as Quinn drew closer. 'You alone, hero?'

'I've got ten men right outside.'

The gun slammed against the side of Mitch's head, felling him to his knees.

'Liar! One geezer might sneak up on me, but never a whole bunch. No – I reckon you're all alone, rancher. OK, now you get up there and bring down the dinero . . . might as well make yourself useful.'

With blood streaming from his temple, Mitch found the way leading up to the ledge where the real lean-to had been built butting on to the cliff wall. There was a cot and a rusted cookpot sitting on a cold fire beneath a stone overhang. Countless cigarette butts had been ground into the rocks and earth. Almost cosy here – if you didn't mind living rough. His gaze narrowed. Lying carelessly against a peeled-pole upright was a sturdy leather valise, buckled up and bulging expensively with the initials R.C.B. stencilled on the side. Rock Creek Bank.

A wave of bitterness swept over him as he stood unmoving. Ever since the start of the manhunt he'd nurtured a strong hope that somehow the outlaw and the loot both might one day somehow tumble into his lap. Of course he'd also been aware he might get killed in the attempt. But he had never envisioned finding the money with a killer's Colt aimed at his heart.

As he started down with the sack the other nodded mockingly.

'Well done, Mitch. I thought you might've tried something really clever, which would mean I'd have to shoot you. Naturally I don't want to get to raising any shooting racket, but don't rely on that if you get to any fancy notions. Play straight and we'll get to hell and gone off this Range and then I'll set you loose when I'm safe. Otherwise you're dead meat.'

'The man you murdered in the canyon was a fine citizen, you butchering bastard.'

'Tell me about it later.'

Quinn gestured towards the fissure with the gun. 'You first, hero.'

Mitch felt like a defeated old man, dull and bereft of either spirit or ideas as he led the way through. The moment he'd looked up to see Quinn grinning down at him over a naked gun he'd realized how foolish he had been to believe he might be capable of dealing with such an outlaw should he eventually get to track him down.

Cody Quinn belonged to a rare and deadly breed, while he was just a simple horse rancher. Not for a moment did he think he would survive even if they did get clear of the Range now. The other's smile and amiable manner didn't deceive. He'd tracked his man and Quinn resented it.

So he would kill him.

It was what killers did.

He found the plateau deserted when he finally pushed his way out through the oak branches.

The outlaw propped and gaped on seeing Lobo standing nearby.

'Well damn my soul if this ain't an omen of good luck for yours truly, and then some! Hiya, old hoss – and didn't we have some times? And now we are gonna have more. You will love Mexico this time of year. Am I ever glad to see your big, old, ugly hammerhead again, pard. Why? you might ask. On account we were always the same breed you and me, right?'

Quinn stepped towards the dun, perhaps momentarily touched by genuine emotion. He was still holding a cocked gun and was fully alert, yet to Mitch's quick eye, marginally less so than he'd been before sighting the stallion. And as Quinn shot a glance over his shoulder at him before reaching out to pat the stallion's neck, something reckless and desperate overtook him and he realized fatalistically that dying fighting rather than waiting to be shot down in cold blood had to be better than having no chance at all.

There was, after all, one hell of a lot in life for a shirt-tail rancher with a wife, a home and a bottlenosed broomtail to live for – if there was one slim chance in hell that he might do it.

He swung the satchel with all his might in a whistling arc.

It struck Cody flush and knocked him clear off his feet.

Mitch dived headlong, both hands grabbing for the gun arm as the outlaw hit ground but immediately began to bounce back up like something made of India rubber.

With all his strength Mitch threw a headbutt that split Cody's brow open almost from nose to hairline. But the tremendous impact of that blow only seemed to galvanize the man into violent response. He drove a knee into the groin then smashed to the side of the head with his gun as Mitch got his fingers to the .45 in his belt, which fell free to earth as he reeled backwards.

He was a dead man.

Mitch saw it in the outlaw's eyes as, weaving like a drunk and spitting blood and curses, the man snarled a hideous curse and the gun was glittering like a live thing in his fist, sweeping up, homing in on him, ready to spew fire and lead at him and blot out his life as though it had never existed.

The scream jolted both men.

It sounded deafeningly shrill and seemed to hang in the air even as Lobo's dusty dun bulk reared high on its hind legs in back of the gunman, iron forehoofs boxing the air, the whites of the eyes turning murderous yellow as Quinn twisted, saw the pumping legs and tried to duck. Instead he was instantly struck down the side of the head with a brutal double blow of rock-hard forefeet that smashed his shoulder and felled him to earth.

Mitch did not remember diving for his own gun in the dust, was barely aware he'd grabbed hold of it as he instinctively rolled aside when Quinn's gun blasted at Lobo with a head-slamming crash of sound.

Mitch saw his chance.

With his Colt held two-handed at arm's length before him, he jerked the trigger in the instant that the dazed and bleeding outlaw twisted his way, his face demonic in its

154

fury, firing before he had a target to fire at.

Mitch's gun answered with a terrible double roar of sound that rocked the world.

And the killer who grinned was smiling no more as he lay looking like a terrible dead child in the strange light.

Mitch Reece sagged back upon the bulging satchel, staring up at the horse with an expression of wonder, relief and something more.

There was a full moon that night a month later. It rose pure yellow out of Shattuck Range, then turned white. The ranch stood beneath it with the fall grass silvered, the trees dark and heavy etched against the sky.

The wind came after dusk. It brushed across the face of the rangeland and started the wolves howling farther back towards Mount Monroe. Ragged cloud scudded across the sky and the scents of the wild places floated down over meadow, pasture, range, river and the home acres where all lay peaceful and asleep save for the tall figure leaning against the horseyard gate with a cigarette in hand and the hammerheaded horse on the other side.

There was something totally different about this night that had brought Mitch out under that white midnight moon; something that had caused Lobo to cross to him and to toss his ragged mane and whicker each time the breeze changed directions.

All was well on Mustang Ranch, yet there was an indefinable something in the very air which held man and beast together, silent and listening for every night sound; the stir of tiny mice feet in the grass, the lonesome hoot of an owl, something rustling high in the tall trees.

Eventually they heard what the something was – a sound which both had heard already without knowing it, but realizing intuitively now that they were both waiting to hear it repeated.

A slow drumbeat arose from beyond the trees and higher up somewhere along the misting, moonwashed slopes of the ranges.

He knew that sound, as did the stallion.

It was the distant yet ever-rising beat of hundreds of hoofs striking ground in a relentless onrushing rhythm.

For the first time in two years the mountain mustangs were avoiding the higher and now colder regions of the rugged Shattucks to come instead flowing across the higher regions of the Esmeralda County rangelands. They flowed in a river of pure grace and pulsing life to sweep across the sleeping rangelands county, driven by an instinct they didn't understand . . . but which Mitch Reece the horseman understood only too well.

From out of somewhere, everywhere or no place in particular within the far recesses of the great land they came running, heads held high and eyes rolling white. They were the wild mustang kings and queens and coltish pretenders running with that swinging double-beat stride mustangs favoured for covering maximum distance with minimum effort. The beat, the surge, the tempo and the tireless energy of their seemingly unstoppable night-flight carried them on like mythical creatures seen in a dream through that night, as it had done throughout the long centuries of America's horse empire.

Mitch knew immediately that he had always somehow known this night and everything it implied would come, and why.

They were coming for him.

Their champion.

It was time.

The rising sound became resonant and almost hypnotic as it grew louder. But Mitch Reece was more acutely aware of what was taking place directly behind his shoulder now, knew that when he turned his head he would see Lobo watching with the look he dreaded, yet had known for some time must surely come. When he finally looked he saw the stallion quivering in every sleek inch, big dark head held high, every sense alert.

Then their glances locked and Mitch read clearly now what he'd first sensed that night in the Shattucks when Quinn had died, and that wild mustang pair had appeared against the moon above them.

Lobo had heard it, felt it and breathed it that night – the call of the wild. The friendship of man and horse had been strong and true. But although the proud mustang king had willingly submitted to a kind master and the ways of the valley dwellers, in his heart he remained what he'd always been, and now instinct, nostalgia and something more was calling him back to the life he'd been born to and to which he could now return.

Mitch's hand raised the bar-board and the gate swung inwards. Lobo quivered and drew nearer. Touching. And in that wordless instant man and horse were closer than ever before, and in that same instant the stud whickered just the once, reared high, then ran.

He watched him merge with the seemingly endless flow of outlaw horses which was now streaming abreast the headquarters out by the horse corrals and, in minutes that seemed like mere moments to the motionless figure at the corral gate, they were gone, wheeling swiftly away upwards now they had gotten what they came for, vanishing into the embrace of the dark mountains and the high country.

Adios, partner.

It was a long time before Mitch returned to the house. He did not speak as he sat in the darkened front room over-looking the Shattuck Range with the last cigarette of the day between his fingers, but Mary heard him anyway. She came to him and slipped her arm across his shoulder.

'Is everything all right, Mitch?'

'Things . . . things have never been better . . . or righter, if there's such a word, honey. . . .' he said, envisioning the great horse streaking away into the night . . . running as he'd been born to do. . . .

And high on the plateau now, Lobo ran swiftly and freely, turning his hammerhead to look over the herd blanketing the land beside him, their backs rising and falling as regularly as the waves of the ocean. His triumphant scream tore through the night and higher up a big lobo wolf howled in reply into the sky. A pretty white-socked filly worked her way alongside him and they were racing, racing for joy and for freedom, running tirelessly for just as far as sinew, heart and spirit could carry them. And then, because of what they were and the pride they carried in their hearts, perhaps even another mile beyond that limit, or maybe another ten . . . as only true mustangs could.

She would never marry.

Her eastern education qualified her for teaching, which she took up with her parents' full approval, for they worried she might be affected by the death of Cody Quinn, and such a fulfilling profession would surely be good for her. Her reputation flourished and in time she was promoted to inspector of schools which took her all over the county.

She had formed a strong friendship with the Reeces and visited whenever she was in their area. She appeared content, serious and fulfilled and was regarded by many a young man as quite beautiful. It took several of them a long time to accept that she simply wasn't interested in romance.

She returned to Rimfire often over the years. When there she stayed with her parents, and there she would always visit the small, well-kept grave in the cemetery and look across at the big plain building where the feature still known as Cody's Window always attracted the curious.

Everyone from her parents down marvelled at her courage and the remarkable fact that whenever speaking of the boy, as she often did, freely and without a tear, she seemed to speak as if he were still alive.

She would never really grieve.

For they had been so close, and he so tender and loving and always so brimfull of life and joy when with her, that greying Carrie Clarke would never, so long as she lived, truly believe that her boy of the blue eyes and tiger heart was dead.